His hand was p̶̶ ̶̶ g to do it. He was goi̶ ̶ ̶ w. If she moved, he would̶ ̶

She prayed for an intervention of some kind. A noise, a voice, even a car horn. She could turn the tiniest distraction into an opportunity. If he even flinched, she could wrench away the gun and demolish CJ with a couple of quick jabs. But the park and its surrounding streets were eerily calm.

Her mind entered into that dream state, in which you process things without quite believing them. This was it? This was the end? This was what it felt like to die?

The barrel shook as he tightened his grip on the trigger. She could see the taut, quivering muscles in his forearm.

The wind had ceased. It seemed there was no one alive on the planet. The night was so silent, she could hear the grinding of his teeth. Or was it her teeth?

His muscles strained, her heart stopped, her eyes squeezed shut. He pulled the trigger.

Don't miss any books in this thrilling new series
from Pocket Books:

FEARLESS™

#1 Fearless
#2 Sam

FEARLESS™

FRANCINE PASCAL

SAM

POCKET BOOKS

An imprint of Simon & Schuster UK Ltd
A Viacom Company
Africa House, 64-78 Kingsway, London WC2B 6AH

Produced by 17th Street Productions,
an Alloy Online, Inc. company
33 West 17th Street, New York, NY 10011

A CIP catalogue record for this book is
available from the British Library

ISBN 0671 03747 1

5 7 9 10 8 6 4

Printed by Cox & Wyman Ltd, Reading, Berkshire

SAM

. . . with
her back to
him and his
gun dug
into her
head,
she was
almost
defenseless.

two

things

IT REALLY WASN'T *THAT* FAR.

Gaia Moore studied the small garden four stories below her window. Well, it wasn't *her* window, exactly. It was one of **Jones** three back windows that belonged to the top floor of the New York City brownstone of George and Ella Niven, her so-called guardians. George was a CIA friend of her dad's from way back when. "Way back when" was typical of the vagueness you got when living with spies and antiterrorist types. They didn't say, "You know, George, the underground assassin I met in Damascus?"

"Gaia?"

Gaia flinched at the voice materializing in her ear. Ella Niven's voice didn't seem to react to air molecules in the normal way. It was breathy and fake intimate, yet carried to the far reaches of the house without losing any of its volume.

"Guy-uhhhhhhh!" Ella bleated impatiently from her dressing room one floor below.

Gaia inched open the window. The window frame was oak, old and creaky with its lead chain and counterweight.

"Gaia? The Beckwiths will be here any minute! Come down now! George asked you to set the table twenty minutes ago!" Now Ella sounded downright whiny.

Gaia could smell bland, watery casserolelike odors

climbing up the stairs and mixing with Ella's strong, spicy perfume. George was a sweetheart and a terrible cook but probably a better cook than potato-brained Ella, who wasn't a sweetheart and never set foot in the kitchen except to whir up a fad-diet shake. The unspoken rule when they had company was that George prepared the food and Ella prepared herself.

Gaia grabbed a five-dollar bill from the top of the bureau and stuffed it in the pocket of her pants. Keys or no keys? That was the question. Mmmm. No keys, Gaia decided.

When the window was open just enough, she climbed out.

Although Ella might think otherwise, Gaia wasn't having dinner with the Beckwiths. They were old State Department people, certain to ask questions about her parents, her past, and her future, her parents, her parents. Gaia could not deal. Why was it that people over the age of thirty felt the need, when confronted with a "young person," to ask so freaking many questions?

Gaia had never agreed to make an appearance tonight. In fact, when Ella had demanded her presence a few hours earlier, Gaia had told Ella she would jump out the window before she'd have dinner with the Beckwiths, and she wasn't kidding.

The autumn air was scented with dry leaves and

frying garlic from the Italian restaurant on West Fourth Street. Distantly Gaia smelled chimney smoke and felt a moment's longing for a different life, when she'd had parents and a pretty house in the Berkshires with a fire in the fireplace every autumn and winter night. That life felt like it belonged to a different person.

She knelt on the narrow windowsill and gripped it with both hands before she lowered herself down. Errg. Her feet tapped blindly for her next toehold while her fingers began to tremble with the exertion of holding up the full weight of her body. Wasn't there a window top or trellis around here somewhere?

At last the toe of her sneaker found purchase in a deeply pitted slab of brownstone. She sank her weight into it, releasing her cramping fingers. And just then, the brownstone cracked under the weight and she fell.

She winced in surprise and annoyance, but she didn't scream. Her mind didn't abandon its rational sequence.

She fell several feet before her hands jammed against the windowsill of a third-floor window, and she miraculously arrested her fall, saving her skull from the slate patio below.

God, that hurt. Angry nerve endings throbbed in her palms, but her heart beat out its same steady rhythm. Air entered her lungs in the same measured breaths as always.

That's why Gaia Moore was different. A freak of nature. Gaia knew that any normal person would have been afraid just then. But she wasn't. She wasn't afraid now, and she wouldn't be ever. She wasn't born with whatever gene it was that made ordinary people feel fear.

It was like something was missing from her genetic tool kit. But doctors weren't sure exactly what it was. They only knew it seemed to affect her reaction to fear. Scientists know the basic setup—there's a master gene that triggers a series of minor genes that in turn control fear reactions. After extensive testing they came up with the theory that one or more of Gaia's genes in that cascade might be inactive or just plain missing.

Something moved on the other side of the window and Gaia squinted to get a better look.

Oh, crap. It was Ella.

Obviously hearing a noise, Ella swiveled her head from the mirror where she was gunking up her eyelashes with mascara and stared into the darkness outside. Ella was both dumb and otherworldly alert. She was self-obsessed but controlling at the same time. Gaia felt her blood start to boil at the mere sight of George's young, plastic wife. Whenever Ella was around, Gaia began to wonder if Mother Nature had given her extra capacity for anger and frustration when she'd left out the capacity for fear.

5

Gaia's fingers were straining so hard on the windowsill, she felt her muscles seizing up. *Go away, Ella. Go away now!*

A less annoying version of Ella would have figured the noise was just a pigeon or something and gotten on with her elaborate primping ritual. But this being the `actual Ella`, she came right over to the window and started to open it. Gaia glanced back over her shoulder, eyeballing the distance between her dangling feet and the patio. It had been reduced to twelve or fifteen feet.

Ella succeeded in throwing open the sash, narrowing her suspicious eyes. "What in the . . . ? Oh, Christ. Is that Gaia? Gaia!"

Gaia raised her head from her painful perch, and their eyes met for a fraction of a second.

It was weird. Ella was vapid and worthless at least nine-tenths of the time, but when she got really mad, her face became sharp and purposeful. Almost vicious. Like if `Barbie` were suddenly possessed by `Atilla the Hun`.

Ella's fingers were only inches from Gaia's. "Oh, hell," Gaia murmured, and let go.

Wump. Her feet took the brunt of the impact, then her knees, then her hands slapped down to steady her. Her knees stung, and she rubbed her hands together, doubting whether she'd ever have feeling in her palms again.

"Gaia! Get back here now!" Ella shrieked.

Gaia peered up momentarily at Ella's white face leaning out of the window. Gaia really hadn't wanted to make a scene. Poor George was never going to hear the end of it.

"Guy-uhhhhhhhhhhhhhhhh!"

Without another look behind her, Gaia ran for the back of the garden. Briefly she paused to glance at the seven fat goldfish swimming in the tiny pond before she leaped over it. She scaled the five-foot garden fence with exceptional grace.

Ella's supersonic voice followed her all the way to Bleecker Street and then dissolved amid the noisy profusion of shops, cafes, and restaurants and the crush of people that made the West Village of Manhattan unique in the world. In a single block you could buy fertility statues from Tanzania, rare Amazonian orchids, a pawned brass tuba, Krispy Kreme doughnuts, or the best, most expensive cup of coffee you ever tasted. It was the doughnuts, incidentally, that attracted Gaia.

She walked past the plastic-wrapped fruit laid out on beds of melting ice and into the deli, where the extravagant salad bar at its center emitted a strong, oily aroma. It was called a salad bar, but it was filled with the least healthful stuff Gaia could imagine (apart from doughnuts, anyway). A trough of deep-fried egg rolls, chicken blobs floating in a sea of pink grease, and some slop vaguely resembling potato salad if you quintupled the mayonnaise. Who ever ate that stuff? Gaia didn't know for sure, but she would have bet her favorite Saucony sneakers that the smelly egg rolls she saw now were exactly the same smelly egg rolls she'd been seeing for the last month.

She made a beeline for the doughnut shelf. Crullers? Cinnamon cakey ones? Powdered sugar? Glazed? Chocolate?

Oh, who was she kidding? She'd been jonesing for a sticky chocolate doughnut all evening. Why pretend any other kind came close? Her mouth was watering as she laid the crumpled five on the counter. The pretty young Korean woman took the bill and gave Gaia her change without really looking up. Somehow, in spite of the fact that they saw each other nearly every day, Gaia and this woman never made any sign of recognition. That was a New York thing—pretend anonymity—and frankly, Gaia liked it. It was perfect, what with Gaia being a not-very-friendly person with a lot of secrets and an embarrassingly large appetite for doughnuts.

Gaia said no thank you to the plastic bag and carried her box of doughnuts in her still-numb hands out of the store, along Bleecker Street toward Seventh Avenue. She figured if you weren't woman enough to carry your doughnuts with pride, you shouldn't be eating them.

Her feet went into auto-walk. They knew their way to Washington Square Park by now. That was her favorite place to eat doughnuts or do just about anything. She chose the perfect park bench, clean and quiet, and sat under a canopy of red-turning leaves that carved the glowing night sky into lace. Hungrily she tore open the box.

Yum.

This moment suddenly contained the entire universe. Hell was eating George's food, watching Ella flirt shamelessly with Mr. Beckwith, and fielding questions about her parents she couldn't imagine answering. This doughnut, this bench, and this sky, on the other hand, were heaven.

"DON'T MOVE."

No Bullet

Okay. Gaia's pupils sped to the corners of her eyes, but she didn't turn her head. Okay, it felt very much like the cold barrel of a gun pressed against her neck. Okay, if Gaia were to feel fear, now would be an obvious time.

The drying leaves were rustling sweetly overhead, the picturesque little puddles cast the glow of the streetlamps back up into the sky, but there wasn't a

9

soul in sight besides the heavy-breathing, perspiring young man crushing the gun into her trapezius muscle.

He was standing behind the bench, but she could make out enough of him through her straining peripheral vision to recognize the nasty little hoodlum she'd seen in the park many times. His name was CJ Somethingorother. She'd not only beaten up his friends but identified him in a police lineup two weeks before as the gang member who'd stabbed Heather Gannis in the park. It didn't tax her imagination to think of why he wanted to scare her. Even hurt her. But kill her?

"Don't freakin' move an inch, bitch."

She sighed. She glanced longingly at her box of doughnuts.

"I *mean* it!"

Ouch. Jesus, he was going to puncture her flesh with the goddamned thing.

He was breathing heavily. He smelled like he'd been drinking. "I know you killed Marco, you sick bitch. And you're gonna pay."

Gaia swallowed hard. Suddenly the doughnut was a bitter clump in her mouth that she couldn't choke down. This guy's voice didn't carry the usual stupid bravado. He wasn't just trying to feel like a man.

Sweat trickled from his hand down the barrel of the gun.

He was dead serious, partly scared, maybe crazy.

Gaia had wondered what had become of Marco. He was a vain, annoying loudmouth, the most conspicuous of the thuggy neo-Nazi guys who contaminated the park. She could tell from the new graffiti she'd seen around the fountain that one of their number was dead.

Now it made sense. Marco was gone, and his boys believed Gaia killed him. That wasn't good news for her. Gaia felt sure there was any number of people who would have wanted to kill Marco.

"I didn't kill Marco," she said in a low, steady voice.

"Bullshit." CJ dragged the gun roughly from her neck to her temple. "Don't mess with me. I know what you did. That's how come you're gonna die."

She could feel her pulse beating against the dead, blunt metal.

CJ steadied the gun with both hands, breathing in deeply.

Oh, God. This was bad. Gaia eased her left hand along the thickly painted wooden slats of the bench.

"Don't move!" he bellowed.

Gaia froze, cringing with pain at the pressure of the gun against her head. A surge of anger ripped through her veins, but as badly as she wanted to break his neck, she recognized that in this position, with her back to him and his gun dug into her head, she was almost defenseless.

She tried to subdue her anger before she opened her mouth.

"CJ, don't do it," she said tightly. "It's a mistake. You're wasting your time here—"

"Shut *up!*" he screamed. "Don't say *any*thing!"

His hand was poised on the trigger. He was going to do it. He was going to kill her right here, right now. If she moved, he would just kill her sooner.

She prayed for an intervention of some kind. A noise, a voice, even a car horn. She could turn the tiniest distraction into an opportunity. If he even flinched, she could wrench away the gun and demolish CJ with a couple of quick jabs. But the park and its surrounding streets were eerily calm.

Her mind entered into that dream state, in which you process things without quite believing them. This was it? This was the end? This was what it felt like to die?

The barrel shook as he tightened his grip on the trigger. She could see the taut, quivering muscles in his forearm.

The wind had ceased. It seemed there was no one alive on the planet. The night was so silent, she could hear the grinding of his teeth. Or was it her teeth?

His muscles strained, her heart stopped, her eyes squeezed shut. He pulled the trigger.

Her mind was in free fall. Perfectly blank. Then, like the burst of a firecracker, came a searing moment of understanding and regret, so complete and profound it shouldn't have been able to fit into a small fraction of a second—

Click.

What was that?

She turned her head. She realized her whole body was shaking. CJ looked just as shocked as he stared at the gun.

It hadn't fired. There was no bullet lodged in her head.

Not yet, anyway. Thank God CJ was an incompetent cave boy. Now, if she didn't get off her butt quick, she'd lose the only chance she had to save it. She shot up to her feet, grabbed CJ by the arm that held the gun, and used it to flip the bastard right over her shoulder. His body smacked hard against the pavement. The gun skidded off the path and into the brush.

She stared at his seizing body for a second. Under normal circumstances she would have stayed to pummel him like he deserved, but tonight she was too genuinely freaked out. She needed to get out of there. Her brains, thankfully, were still safely in her skull, but her emotions were splattered on the pavement.

Gaia ran. She ran as fast and gracefully as a doe. But not so fast that she didn't hear the tortured voice screaming behind her.

"I will kill you! I swear to *God* I will kill you!"

Tonight, as I sat on the park bench waiting for my head to explode, I had one moment of clarity in which I learned two things.

1) I have to find my dad.

I just have to. As angry as I am, as much as I hate him for abandoning me on the most awful, vulnerable day of my life, I don't want to die without seeing him one more time. I don't know what I'll say to him. But there's something I want to know, and I feel like if I can look in his eyes—just for a moment—I'll know what his betrayal meant and whether there's any love or trust, even the possibility of it, between us.

2) I have to have sex.

Oh, come on. Don't act so shocked. I'm seventeen years old. I know the rules about being safe. If my life weren't in very immediate jeopardy, maybe I would let it wait for the exact right time. But let's face it—I may not be around next week, forget about happily ever after. Besides, I've been through a lot of truly awful things in my life, so why should I die without getting to experience one of the few great ones?

Who am I going to have sex with? Do you have to ask?

All right, I have an answer. In that moment, when my fragile mindset was shattered, the face I saw belonged to Sam Moon. Granted, he hates me. Granted, he has a girlfriend. Granted, his girlfriend hates me even more. But I'll find a way. 'Cause he's the one. I can't say why; he just is.

I wish I could convince myself that CJ wouldn't make good on his threat. But I heard his voice. I saw his face. I know he'll do any crazy thing it takes.

I won't go down easy. But I'd be stupid not to prepare for the worst.

Am I afraid? No. I'm never afraid. But the way I see it, dying without knowing love would be a tragedy.

She hated
that pale
blond hair,
a color
you **desperate**
rarely saw
on a person
over the age
of three.

"YOU SOUND WEIRD."

"How do you mean?" Gaia asked.

"I don't know. You just do. You're talking fast or something," Ed said as he clenched the portable phone between his shoulder and his ear and eased himself from his desk chair to his wheelchair.

Ed Fargo was honest with Gaia, and Gaia was honest with Ed. He appreciated that about their relationship. With most girls he knew, girls like Heather, there were many mystifying levels of bullshit. With Gaia he could just tell her exactly what he was thinking.

Ed's mind briefly flashed on the hip-hugging green corduroys Gaia was wearing in Mr. McAuliff's class today.

Well, actually, not *everything* he was thinking. There was a certain category of thing he couldn't tell her about. That's why it was often easier talking with her on the phone, because then he couldn't see her, which meant he had fewer of those thoughts he couldn't tell her about.

"I had a bad night. That's probably why," Gaia said.

Ed wheeled himself down the shabbily carpeted hallway of his family's small apartment. Family photographs lined the walls on both sides, but Ed didn't seem to see them anymore. "A bad night how?" he asked.

18

"I almost got shot in the head."

Ed made a sound somewhere between laughter and choking on a chicken bone. "You w-what?"

That was another thing about Gaia. She was always surprising. Though too often in an upsetting way.

Gaia let out her breath. "Oh, God. Where to start. You know that guy CJ?"

Ed slowed his chair to a stop and clenched the armrests with his hands. "The one who slashed Heather? Isn't he in jail?" he asked with a sick feeling in his stomach.

"I guess he got out on bail or something," Gaia said matter-of-factly. "Anyway, CJ's friend Marco is dead, and he thinks I killed him."

Ed groaned out loud. How had his life taken such a turn? Before he'd first laid love-struck eyes on Gaia in the hallway outside physics class, he wouldn't have believed he would ever have a conversation like this.

"Marco is dead? Are you sure?"

"Only from what CJ told me."

Ed sighed. The really crazy thing was, in the brief time he'd known Gaia, so many violent and alarming things had happened, this wasn't so staggeringly out of the ordinary.

"Hey, Gaia? If trouble is a hungry great white shark, then you're a liquid cloud of chum."

Gaia's laugh was easy and comforting. "That's a beautiful image. I love it when you get poetic."

19

Ed resumed his roll down the hallway and into the galley kitchen. His late evening phone reports from Gaia, distressing as they sometimes were, had become as precious a ritual as his eleven o'clock milk shake.

"So tell me," Ed prodded, hoisting himself up a few inches with one arm to reach the ice cream in the freezer. "Tell me how it happened."

"Okay. I was sitting in the park, minding my own business—"

"Eating doughnuts," Ed supplied.

"Yes, Ed, eating doughnuts, when that loser came up from behind and shoved a gun into my neck."

"Jesus."

"I didn't take it seriously at first. But it turns out this guy is half crazed and deadly serious."

"So what happened?" Ed asked, milk shake momentarily forgotten.

Gaia sighed. "He actually pulled the trigger. I thought I was dead—a wild experience, by the way. It turned out he must have loaded the gun in a hurry because there was no bullet in at least one of the chambers. I took that opportunity to throw him."

Ed's mind was spinning. "Throw him?"

"You know, like flip him."

"Oh, right," he said.

"You're making fun of me again," Gaia said patiently.

20

Ed shook his head in disbelief. "I'm not, Gaia. It's just . . . you blow my mind."

"Well, speaking of, I think this guy CJ is dead set on killing me. I'm scared he's really going to do it," Gaia said.

"You're scared?" Ed asked a little nervously. Having seen Gaia in action, he would have imagined it would take more than a pimply white supremacist with a borrowed gun to hurt Gaia. It would take something more on the order of a hydrogen bomb. But if Gaia was scared, well, he had to take that seriously.

"Figure of speech. I'm scared *abstractly,*" Gaia explained.

Ed rocked a tall glass on the counter. "Gaia, you worry me here."

"Don't worry," Gaia reassured him. "I mean, think about it. CJ is kind of a moron, and I happen to be okay at self-defense."

Ed felt reassured. That last part was an understatement to rival "Marilyn Manson is an unusual guy." He could hear Gaia thumping her heel against her metal desk. He realized the ice cream was melting and spreading along the countertop. He absently scooped some of it into the blender.

Prrrrrrrrrrrrr.

"Ed! I hate when you run the blender when we're talking," Gaia complained loudly.

"Sorry," he said. By the time she finished

complaining, the milk shake was frothy and smooth. That was part of the ritual.

"I don't want to die," she said resolutely. "You know why?"

"Why?" he asked absently, sucking down a huge mouthful of vanilla shake.

"I haven't had sex yet."

Ed spluttered the mouthful all over his dark blue T-shirt. Cough, cough, cough. "What?"

"I don't want to die before I've had sex."

Cough, cough.

"Right," he said.

"So I need to have sex in the next couple of days, just in case," Gaia added.

Cough, cough, cough, cough, cough, cough, cough, cough, cough, cough—

"Ed? Are you okay? Ed? Is somebody around to give you the Heimlich?"

"N-No," Ed choked out. "I'm (cough, cough) fine."

In fact, he had about four ounces of milk shake puddled in his lung. Could you die of that? Could you drown by breathing in a milk shake? And shit, he'd like to have sex in the next couple of days, too. (Cough, cough, cough.)

"Ed, are you sure you're okay?"

"Yesss," he answered in a weak and gravelly voice.

"So anyway, I was thinking I better do it soon."

"It?"

"Yeah, it. You know, *it*."

"Right. It." Ed felt faint. Milk shake, as it turned out, was much less handy in your veins than, say, oxygen. "So, who . . . uh . . . are you going to do *it* with? Or are you just going to walk the streets, soliciting people randomly?"

"Ed!" Gaia sounded genuinely insulted.

"Kidding," he said feebly, wishing his palms weren't suddenly sweating.

"You don't think anybody's going to want to have sex with me, do you?" Gaia sounded hurt and petulant at the same time.

"Mmrnpha." The noise Ed made didn't resemble an English word. It sounded like it had come from the mouth of a nine-month-old baby.

"Huh?"

"I . . . um . . ." Ed couldn't answer. The truth was, although she made every effort to hide it, Gaia was possibly the most beautiful girl he had ever seen in his life—and that was including the women in the Victoria's Secret catalog, the *SI* swimsuit issue, and that show about witches on the WB. Any straight guy with a live pulse and a thimble full of testosterone would want to have sex with Gaia. But what was Ed going to say? This was *exactly* the category of conversation he couldn't have honestly with her.

"Anyway, I do know who I'm going to do it with," Gaia said confidently.

"Who?" Ed felt his vision blurring.

"I can't say."

Ed definitely wasn't taking in enough oxygen. Good thing he was in a chair because otherwise he'd be lying on the linoleum.

"Why can't you say?" he asked, trying to sound calm.

"Because it's way too awkward," Gaia said.

Awkward? Awkward. What did that imply? Could it mean . . . ? Ed's thoughts were racing. Would it be too crude to point out at this juncture that although his legs were paralyzed, his nether regions were in excellent working condition?

He felt a tiny tendril of hope winding its way into his heart. He beat it back. "Gaia, don't you think you'll need to get past *awkwardness* if you really plan to be doing *it* with this person in the next forty-eight hours?"

"Yeah, I guess." He heard her slam her heel against the desk. "But I still can't tell you."

"Oh, come on, Gaia. You have to."

"I gotta go."

"Gaia!"

"I really do. Cru-Ella needs to use the phone."

"Gaia! Please? Come on! Tell."

"See ya tomorrow."

"Gaia, who? Who, who, who?" Ed demanded.

"You," he heard her say in a soft voice before she hung up the phone.

But as he laid the phone on the counter he knew who'd said the word, and it wasn't Gaia. It was that misguiding, leechlike parasite called hope.

THE TIME HAD COME. HEATHER

One Small Comment

Gannis felt certain of that as she slammed her locker door shut and tucked the red envelope into her book bag. She waited for the deafening late afternoon crowd to clear before striking out toward the bathroom. She didn't feel like picking up the usual half-dozen hangers-on, desperate to know what she was doing after soccer practice.

Okay, time to make her move. She caught sight of Melanie Young in her peripheral vision but pretended she hadn't. She acted like she didn't hear Tannie Deegan calling after her. Once in the bathroom she hid in the stall for a couple of minutes to be sure she wasn't being followed.

Heather usually liked her high visibility and enormous number of friends, but some of those girls were so freakishly *needy* some of the time. It was like if they missed one group trip to the Antique

Boutique, they would never recover. Their clinginess made it almost impossible for Heather to spend one private afternoon with her boyfriend.

Heather dumped her bag in the mostly dry sink and stared at her reflection. She wanted to look her best when she saw Sam. She bent her head so close to the mirror that her nose left a tiny grease mark on the glass. This close, she could see the light freckles splattered across the bridge of her nose and the amber streaks in her light eyes that kept them from being the bona fide true blue of her mother and sisters.

Her pores looked big and ugly from this vantage point. Did Sam see them this way when he kissed her? She pulled away. She got busy rooting through her bag for powder to tame the oil on her forehead and nose and hopefully cover those gaping, yawning pores. She applied another coat of clear lip gloss. For somebody who was supposed to be so beautiful, she sure felt pretty plain sometimes.

She wished she hadn't eaten those potato chips at lunch. She couldn't help worrying that the difference between beauty and hideousness would come down to one bag of salt-and-vinegar chips.

As she swung her bag over her shoulder and smacked open the swinging door, she caught sight of the dingy olive-colored pants and faded black hooded sweatshirt of Gaia Moore. Heather's heart picked up pace, and she felt blood pulsing in her temples.

God, she hated that girl. She hated the way she walked, the way she dressed, the way she talked. She hated that pale blond hair, a color you rarely saw on a person over the age of three. Heather wished the color was fake, but she knew it wasn't.

Heather hated Gaia for dumping scorching-hot coffee all over her shirt a couple of weeks ago and not bothering to apologize. Heather hated Gaia for being friends with Ed Fargo, her ex-boyfriend, and turning him against Heather at that awful party. Heather *really* hated Gaia for failing to warn Heather that there was a guy with a knife in the park, when Heather was obviously headed there.

All of those things were unforgivable. But none of them kept Heather up at night. The thing that kept her up at night was one small, nothing comment made by her boyfriend, Sam Moon.

It happened the day Heather got out of the hospital. Sam was there visiting, as he was throughout those five days. He had disappeared for a few minutes, and when he got back to her room, Heather asked him where he'd been. He said, "I ran into Gaia in the hallway." That was all. Afterward, when Heather quizzed him, Sam instantly claimed to dislike Gaia. Like everybody else, he said it was partly Gaia's fault that Heather got slashed in the first place.

But there was something about Sam's face when he said Gaia's name that stuck in Heather's mind and wouldn't go away.

Heather's mind returned again to the card floating in her bag. She sorted through the bag and pulled it out. She needed to check again that the words seemed right. That the handwriting didn't look too girly and stupid. That the phrasing didn't seem too ... desperate.

She'd find Sam in the park playing chess with that crazy old man, as he often did on Wednesday afternoons. And if not, she'd go on to his dorm and wait for him there. She'd hand him the card, watch his face while he read it, and kiss him so he'd know she meant it.

She was in love with Sam. This Saturday marked their six-month anniversary. He was the best-looking, most intelligent guy she knew. She loved the fact that he was in college.

She had made this decision with her heart. Sam was sexy. Sam was even romantic sometimes. He wasn't a guy you let get away.

So why, then, as she wrote the card, was she thinking not of Sam, but of Gaia?

> *Dear Sam,*
> *These last six months have been the best of my life. Sorry to be corny, but it's true. So I wanted to celebrate the occasion with a very*

special night. I'll meet you at your room at eight on Saturday night and we'll finally do something we've been talking about doing for a long time. I know I said I wanted to wait, but I changed my mind.

You are the one, and now is the time.

Love and kisses (all over),

Heather

He smiled at
her. This **lonely**
time it
was sweet, **hearts**
open, real.

"THAT STUPID PUNK WILL NOT KILL
Gaia!" he thundered.
"Do you understand?"

He strode to the far
end of the loft apart-
ment and kicked over a
side table laden with coffee mugs. Most rolled;
one shattered. One of the two bodyguards who
hovered in the background came forward to clean
them up.

He spun on Ella. He hated her face at moments like
this. *"Do you understand?"*

"Of course I understand," she said sullenly. "I wasn't
expecting her to climb out the window," she added in a
scornful mumble.

"Learn to *expect* it!" he bellowed. "Gaia is *not* an
ordinary girl! Haven't you figured that *out?"*

Ella's eyes darted with reptilian alertness, but she
wisely kept her mouth shut.

"Gaia is no use to me dead. I will not let it happen.
I don't care how crazy the girl is. I don't care if she
throws herself in the path of a bus. I will *not* let it happen!" He was ranting now. He couldn't stop now if he
wanted to. He'd always had a bad temper.

"Show me the pictures," he demanded of Ella.

Reluctantly Ella came near and put the pile in his
hands.

He studied the first one for a long time. It was Gaia sitting alone on a park bench. Her face was tipped down, partly obscured by long, pale hair. Her gray sweatshirt was sagging off one shoulder. Her long legs were crossed, and a little burst of light erupted from the reflective patch on her running shoe. A box of doughnuts sat open on the bench next to her.

Her gesture and manner were so familiar to him, he felt an odd stirring in his chest. Though Gaia was undeniably beautiful with her graceful, angular face, she didn't resemble Katia. Katia had dark glossy hair, brown eyes flecked with orange, and a smaller, more voluptuous build.

In the next picture Gaia's head was raised, and in the shadow behind her was the boy pointing the gun at her head. The boy looked agitated, his eyes wild. Yet Gaia's face was impossibly calm. He brought the picture close. Remarkable. Utterly fascinating. There was no fear in those wide-set blue eyes. He would know. He had a great gift for detecting fear.

Gaia was indeed everything he had heard about her. All the more reason why he could not accept another ridiculous close call like this one.

He glanced at the next picture. The boy was leaning in closer, his face clenched as he prepared to pull the trigger.

"Keep that boy and his stupid friends away from her," he barked at Ella.

"Yes," she mumbled.

"He will not get that gun anywhere near Gaia!"

"Yes, sir."

He glared at Ella with withering eyes. "Hear me now, Ella. If *anyone* kills Gaia Moore, it will be me."

Ella's gaze was cast to the ground.

He studied the next picture in the pile. This one showed Gaia standing in all her ferocious glory, flipping that pitiful boy over her shoulder. Her face was wonderfully alert, intense. She was magnificent. More than he could have hoped for.

No, Gaia didn't resemble Katia, he decided as he studied the lovely face in the picture. Gaia resembled him.

SHE PROBABLY WOULDN'T EVEN BE

there. Why would she? She'd be avoiding him if she had any sense.

Sam Moon hurried into Washington Square Park with his physics textbook tucked under his arm. Then again, if *he* had any sense, he'd be avoiding *her*. Instead he was darting around the park at all hours like some kind of timid stalker, hoping to catch a glimpse of her.

Like a Drug

He approached the shaded area where the chess tables sat, surveying them almost hungrily. No. She wasn't there. It verged on ridiculous, the physical feeling of disappointment that radiated through his abdomen.

He kept his distance, reviewing his options. He didn't want to plunge right into chess world because then all his cohorts would see him and he'd be stuck for at least a game or two. And he'd found out the hard way that when Gaia was on his mind (and when wasn't she?), he was a lot worse at chess.

Maybe she had come and gone already. Maybe she'd caught sight of him from a distance and taken off. Maybe she really did hate him—

"Moon?"

Sam practically leaped right out of his clothes. He spun around. "Jesus, Renny, you scared the crap out of me."

Renny smiled in his open, friendly way. He was a wiry-looking, barely adolescent Puerto Rican kid who was quickly becoming a lethal chess player. "You looking for Gaia?"

Sam's face fell. Was his head made of glass? Was his romantic torment, which he believed to be totally private and unique, available for public display? Was everybody who knew him talking and snickering about it? Even the chess nerds, who wouldn't ordinarily notice if you'd had one of your legs amputated?

"No," Sam lied defensively. "Why?"

"I figure you're getting tired of whipping the rest of us. Gaia could probably get a game off you, huh?"

Sam studied Renny's face for signs of cleverness or mockery. No. Renny wasn't being a wise guy. He wasn't suddenly Miss Lonely Hearts. Renny was thinking the same way he always thought, like a chess player.

Sam let out a breath. He tried to relax the crackling nerve synapses in his neck and shoulders. There was a word for this: *paranoia*.

"Yeah," Sam said in a way he hoped was nonchalant. "Maybe one or two. If she was on her game."

"Yeah," Renny said, "she's unbelievable." Renny's eyes got a little glassy, but Sam could tell he was fantasizing about Gaia's stunning end play, not about her lips or her eyes.

Unlike Sam.

"Yeah," Sam repeated awkwardly.

"See you." Renny clapped him on the back agreeably and waded into chess world. Sam watched Renny take the first open seat across from Mr. Haq, whose taxicab was predictably parked (illegally) at the nearest curb. That was the downside of playing Mr. Haq. If the cops came, he abandoned the game and put his cab back into action. And no matter how badly you were creaming him, Mr. Haq would always refer to it afterward as "an undecided match."

Sam found his way to a nearby bench with a good

view of the chess area. He opened his physics book, lame prop that it was.

What had happened to his resolution to forget about Gaia? He'd decided to put her out of his mind for good and focus all of his romantic energy on Heather, but Gaia was like a drug. She was in his blood, and he couldn't get her out. He was a junkie, an addict. He knew Gaia was bad for him. He knew she'd undermine his commitments and basically ruin his life. But he obsessed about her, anyway. Was there a twelve-step program for an addiction like this? Gaia Worshipers Anonymous?

He remembered that antidrug slogan that had scared him as a kid. *This is your brain.* He pictured the sizzling egg. *This is your brain thinking of Gaia.*

Clearly his decisions, vows, determinations, and oaths to forget Gaia weren't enough. Maybe it was time to try a different tack.

What if he attempted to relate to her as a normal person? Just talk to her about everyday things like school and extracurricular activities and stuff like that? Maybe he could demystify the whole relationship.

Maybe he and Gaia could even have a meal together. You couldn't easily idolize a girl while she was stuffing her face. She would probably order something he hated like lox or coleslaw. She would chew too loudly or maybe wear a bit of red cabbage on her front tooth for a while. Maybe she would spit a little when she talked. Afterward she would have bad breath or maybe a grease spot on her pants, and voilà. Obsession over.

Yes. This was a practical idea. Demystification.

Because after all, although Gaia came off as a pretty extraordinary person on the outside, on the inside she was just the same as anybody else.

. . . right?

SHE WAS A MESS.

She was a nightmare.

She should have her license to be female revoked.

Gaia turned around to look at her backside in the slightly warped mirror that hung on the back of the door to her room.

Earlier that day she'd picked up a pair of capri pants off the sale rack at the Gap in an effort to look cute and feminine. Instead she looked like the Incredible Hulk right after he turns green and bursts out of his clothing.

What kind of shoes were you supposed to wear with these things? Definitely not boots, as she could plainly see in the mirror. Was it too late in the year to wear flip-flops?

Sam was not going to fall in love with her. He was going to take one look and run screaming in the opposite direction. Either that or laugh uncontrollably.

Why was she torturing herself this way? In her ordinary life she managed to pull off the functional style of a person who didn't care. She had no money, which occasionally resulted in the coincidental coolness of thrift shop dressing.

But now that Gaia actually cared, she had turned herself into a neurotic, insecure freak show.

Caring was to be deplored and avoided. Hadn't she learned that by now?

She stripped off the pants and pulled on her least-descript pair of jeans. She pulled a nubbly sweater the color of oatmeal over her head.

Better ugly than a laughingstock. That was Gaia's new fashion motto.

She had to get out of the house before Ella sauntered in and recognized the beaded necklace Gaia had "borrowed." Ella was a whiny, dumb bimbo, but she had a nose for fashion trends. Gaia had every intention of returning the necklace before it was missed, so why cause a big fuss by asking?

Gaia thundered down the three flights of stairs, slammed the painted oak-and-glass door behind her, turned her key in the lock, and struck out for the park.

And to think she'd come home after school to work on her appearance.

She hurried past the picture-perfect row houses. Lurid red geraniums still exploded in the window boxes. Decorative little front fences cast long shadows in the late day sun, putting Gaia's shadow in an attenuated, demented-looking prison.

After a few blocks, Gaia suddenly paused as the sound of heavy guitar music blared through an open basement window, followed by a raspy tenor voice. "framed/you set me up, set me out and/blamed/you tore me up, tore me down and/chained/you tied me up, tied me down and . . . " It was that band again—Fearless. For a fleeting moment Gaia wanted to shout through the window and ask them where they got their bizarrely Gaia-centric name, but she had to keep moving.

She didn't have much time. CJ probably wasn't crazy enough to open fire on her in daylight, but once the sun got really low, she had to be ready for it, especially hanging around the park. How typical of her new life in the biggest city in the United States that the guy she wanted to seduce and the guy who wanted to shoot her hung out in exactly the same space.

Her stomach started to churn as she got close. What was she going to say to Sam?

"Hi, I know you have a girlfriend and don't like me at all, but do you want to have sex?"

On the one-in-ten-billion chance that he agreed to

her insane scheme, what then? They couldn't just do it on a park bench.

Suddenly the actual, three-dimensional Sam, sitting on a bench with a clunky-looking textbook open on his lap, replaced the Sam in her mind.

Oh, crap. Was it too late? Had he seen her?

"Gaia?"

That would mean yes.

Swallow. "Hi." She tried out a friendly smile that came off more like the expression a person might make when burning a finger on the top of the toaster.

He stood up, his smile looking equally pained. "How's it going?"

She hooked her thumbs in the front pockets of her pants. "Oh, fine. Fine." What was she? A farmer?

"Yeah?"

"Yeah."

"Great."

Oh, this was awful. This come-hither Gaia was a complete disaster. Why couldn't she be cute and flirty *and* have a personality?

He was clearly at a loss. "Do you, uh . . . want to play a game of chess?"

She would have agreed to pull out her toenails to escape this awkward situation.

"Yeah, sure, whatever," she said lightly. God, what a wordsmith she was.

"Or we could just, like, take a walk. Or something."

"Great. Sure," she said. Had her vocabulary shrunk to four words?

"Or we could even sit here for a couple of minutes."

"Yeah," she proclaimed.

"Fine," he countered.

"Great," she said.

They both stayed standing.

This was pathetic. How was she possibly going to have sex with him when simply sitting on the same bench involved a whole choreography of commitment?

She sat. There.

He sat, too.

Well, this was progress.

She crossed her legs and inadvertently brushed the heel of his shoe. With lightning-fast-reflex speed they both swung their respective feet to opposite sides of the bench.

Or not.

Gaia studied Sam's face in profile. It made her a little giddy to realize what a hunk he was. A classic knee weakener. He belonged on television or in a magazine ad for cologne. What was he doing sitting near *her*?

He looked up and caught her staring (slack jawed) at him. She quickly looked away. She pressed her hand, palm down, on the bench and realized her pinky was touching the outer edge of his thigh. *Uh-oh.*

Should she move it? Had he noticed? Did he think she had done it on purpose? Suddenly she had more feeling, more nerve endings (billions and billions at least) in her pinky than she ever thought possible. All of the awareness in her body was crammed into that pinky.

Now it felt clammy and weirdly twitchy. A pinky wasn't accustomed to all this attention. Did Sam feel it twitching? That would be awful. He'd think it was some kind of lame come-on. Either that or she'd lost muscle control.

Well, actually, this *was* some kind of lame come-on and she *had* lost control.

The problem was, if she took away her pinky, he would know she noticed that she was touching him, and that would be embarrassing, too.

He moved his leg. Suddenly Gaia's pinky was touching cold, lonely, uncharged air. She felt the piercing sting of rejection. Jerk. Loser. She was ready to give up on the whole project.

Then he moved it back and practically covered her entire pinky. Oh, faith! Love! Destiny! Could she propose to him right there?

He smiled at her. This time it was sweet, open, real.

Her stomach rolled. She smiled back, fervently

hoping it didn't look like a grimace and that her teeth didn't look yellow.

She heard a noise behind her. She jerked up her head.

She realized that the sun had dipped below the Hudson River and the streetlamps were illuminated. Oh, no. Could it be? Already?

She had to go. Fast. She wasn't going to turn into a pumpkin, but she was very likely going to get shot in the head. That could easily put a damper on this fragile, blossoming moment.

The sound resolved itself into a footstep, and a person appeared. It wasn't CJ, but just the same, it put an end to the encounter as powerfully as a bullet.

It was Heather. The girlfriend.

Her adrenaline
was pumping
now. Her
muscles were
buzzing with
intensity.
She was an
easy target
this close.

**cold
blood**

THERE WERE MOMENTS IN LIFE WHEN

words failed to convey your thoughts. There were moments when your thoughts failed to convey your feelings. Then there were moments when even your feelings failed to convey your feelings.

Cunning Intelligence

This was one of those, Heather realized as she gaped at Sam and Gaia Moore sitting on the park bench together.

They weren't kissing. They weren't touching. They weren't even talking. But Sam and Gaia could have been doing the nasty right there on the spot, and it wouldn't have carried the intimacy of this tentative, nervous, neurotic union she now witnessed between them.

Maybe she was imagining it, Heather considered. Maybe it was a figment of her own obsessive, jealous mind.

She'd almost rather believe she was crazy than that Sam, *her Sam*, was falling in love with Gaia. It was too coincidental, just too cruel to be real. Like one of those Greek tragedies she read for Mr. Hirschberg's class. Gaia was the person she most despised. Sam was the person she loved.

Had she done something to bring this on herself?

What was it the Greek guys always got smacked for? *Hubris,* that was the word—believing you were too good, too strong, invulnerable. The world had a way of teaching you that you weren't invulnerable.

Heather was paralyzed. Anger told her to get between them and make trouble, Pride told her to run away. Hurt told her to cry. Cunning told her to make Sam feel as guilty and small as possible. She waited to hear what Intelligence had to say. It never spoke first, but its advice was usually worth waiting for.

Her mind raced and sorted. Considered and rejected. Then finally, Intelligence piped up with a strategy.

"Sam," Heather stated. Good, firm, steady voice. She stepped around to the front of the bench and faced them straight on.

Sam looked up. Shock, fear, guilt, uncertainty, and regret waged war over his features.

Staring at them, Heather made no secret of her surprise and distress, but she overlaid a brave, tentative, give-them-the-benefit-of-the-doubt smile.

The effect was just as she'd intended. Sam looked like he wished to pluck out both of his eyeballs on the spot.

"Hey, Gaia," Heather said. Her expression remained one of naive, martyrlike confusion.

Gaia looked less sure of herself than Heather had ever seen her before. Gaia cleared her throat, uncrossed her legs, straightened her posture, said nothing. Heather detected a faint blush on her cheeks.

Now Heather looked back at Sam. She applied no obvious pressure, just silence, which always proved the fiercest pressure of all.

"Heather, I—we—you—" Sam looked around, desperate for her to interrupt.

She didn't.

"I was just . . . and Gaia, here . . ."

Heather wasn't going to help him out of this. Let him suffer.

"We were just . . . talking about chess." With that word, Sam regained his footing. He took a big breath. "Gaia is a big chess player, too."

Heather nodded trustingly. "Oh."

Sam looked at his watch. There wasn't a watch. A moment's discomfort. He regrouped again. "I gotta go, though." He stood up. "Physics study group." He offered his textbook as evidence.

"Right," Heather said. "Wait, I have something for you." She fished around in her bag and brought out the red sealed envelope. "Here. I was looking for you because I wanted to give you this." She smiled shyly. She shrugged. "It's kind of stupid, but . . . whatever." Her voice was soft enough to be intimate and directed solely at him.

He had to come two steps closer to take the card

from her hand. This required him to turn his back on Gaia.

Sam glanced at his name, written in flowery cursive, and the heart she'd drawn next to it. When he looked at Heather again, his eyes were pained, uncertain.

He cleared his throat. "Why don't you walk with me, and I'll open it when I get to my dorm?"

Heather nodded brightly. "Okay."

He pressed the card carefully between the pages of his physics book and anchored the book under his arm. Heather took his free hand and laced her fingers through his as she often did, and they started across the park.

Sam said nothing to Gaia. He didn't even cast a backward glance.

But Heather couldn't help herself. She threw a tiny look over her shoulder. Then, without breaking her stride, she planted one fleeting kiss on Sam's upper arm, just the place where her mouth naturally landed on his tall frame. It was a casual kiss, light, one of millions, but undoubtedly a kiss of ownership.

"See ya," Heather said to Gaia, silently thanking Intelligence for dealing her yet another effective strategy.

It was funny, thought Heather. Intelligence and Cunning so often ended up in the same place.

49

WHAT GOOD WAS IT BEING A TRAINED

fighting machine when you couldn't beat the hell out of a loathsome creature like Heather Gannis? Gaia wondered

Not Yet

bitterly as she stomped along the overcrowded sidewalks of SoHo.

What a catty piece of crap Heather was. No, that was too kind. Cats were fuzzy, warm-blooded, and somewhat loyal. Heather was more reptile than mammal—cold-blooded and remote with dead, hooded eyes.

Gaia was supposed to be smart. When she was six years old, her IQ tested so high, she'd been sent to the National Institutes of Health to spend a week with electrodes stuck to her forehead. And yet in Heather's presence Gaia felt like a slobbering idiot. She'd probably misspell her name if put on the spot.

"Oops. Sorry," Gaia mumbled to a man in a beige suit whose shoulder she caught as she crossed Spring Street.

Trendy stores were ablaze along the narrow cobblestoned streets. Well-dressed crowds flowed into the buzzing, overpriced restaurants that Ella always wanted to go to. Gaia strode past a cluster of depressingly hip girls who probably never considered wearing boots with capri pants.

Gaia caught her reflection in the darkened window

of a florist shop. Ick. Blah. Blech. Who let her out on the streets of New York in that sweater? Exactly how fat could her legs look? High time to get rid of the—

Suddenly she caught sight of another familiar reflection. He was behind her, weaving and dodging through the throng, staying close but trying to avoid her notice. His face was beaded with sweat. One of his hands was tucked in his jacket.

Oh, shit. Well, at least you couldn't commit fashion blunders from the grave, could you?

She walked faster. She jaywalked across the street and ducked into a boutique. She wanted to see whether CJ was just keeping tabs on her or whether he intended to kill her immediately.

Gaia blinked in the laboratory-bright shop. The decor was spare, and the clothing was inscrutable. In the midst of all the chrome shelving and halogen lighting there seemed to be about three items for sale, all of them black. It made for poor browsing.

CJ stopped outside. He knew she knew he was there.

"Excuse me, miss." An impatient voice echoed through the stark, high-ceilinged room.

Gaia spun around to see a severe-looking saleslady pinning her to the floor with a suspicious look. Salesladies in SoHo had a sixth sense for whether you could afford anything in their store. It was a superhuman power. It deserved to be investigated on *The X-Files*. This particular woman obviously knew that Gaia couldn't afford even a zipper or sleeve from the place.

"We're closed," the saleslady snapped. Her outfit was constructed of incredibly stiff-looking black material that covered her from her pointy chin to the very pointy tips of her shoes. Gaia couldn't help wondering if she ate breakfast or watched TV in that getup.

"The door was open," Gaia pointed out.

The woman cocked her head and made a sour face. "Apparently so. But we're closed."

"Fine." Gaia glanced through the glass door. CJ was pacing in an area of about two square feet. He was ready to pounce. She was pretty sure that the hand concealed in his roomy jacket held a gun.

"In the future, when you're closed," Gaia offered, trying to bide a little time, "you should consider *locking* your door. It's a common business practice. It not only alerts your customers to the fact that your store is closed but can help reduce crime as well."

"Are you done?" the woman asked, rolling her eyeballs skyward.

"Um, yeah." Gaia glanced out the door reluctantly. It opened outward. The glass was thick and well reinforced.

"Please leave."

Gaia backed up a few feet. "Okay," she said.

One . . . two . . . three . . .

Gaia slammed into the door at full strength.

Just as she'd hoped, the door flew open and caught CJ hard in the face, knocking him backward. She heard his groan of surprise and pain. It gave her the moment she needed to run.

SoHo, with its single-file sidewalks and indignant pedestrians, was not a good place for sprinting.

"Ex*cuse* me!"

"Yo, watch it!"

"What's your problem?"

Gaia left a stream of angry New Yorkers in her wake. "Sorry!" she called out in a blanket apology. It was the best she could do at the moment.

She heard CJ shouting behind her. Then pounding footsteps and the protests of more unhappy pedestrians.

Gaia hung a quick left on Greene Street. She navigated the sidewalk with the deftness of a running back.

She heard screams as CJ (presumably) crashed into a woman with a screechy voice. He was gaining on Gaia. He cared less than she did about thrashing innocent bystanders.

Gaia hooked onto Broome Street and ran west. CJ was just a few yards behind. The street was clotted with traffic, and she needed to cross to the south side, where the sidewalk was clear. The crosswalk was too far. She heard more screams and then a man's voice.

"That kid's got a gun! A *gun!* Everybody down!"

"Damn it!" Gaia muttered. Her adrenaline was pumping now. Her muscles were buzzing with intensity. She was an easy target this close. Now what?

Parked cars were nose to tail at the curb without a break. Gaia pounced on the first parked car she came upon, putting both hands above the driver's side window and vaulting herself onto the roof. She was in full flee mode now, and she didn't have the luxury to care about making a spectacle. Thin metal thundered and buckled under her feet. She surveyed the traffic piled up behind the light. She jumped to the roof of the next-nearest car and picked her way across the street from car to car the way she'd use stones to traverse a river. Cars honked. Cabbies shouted. A shot rang out to her left. Oh, man.

CJ had beaten her to the other side of Broome Street. The idiot was shooting at her in front of hundreds of witnesses. God, she wanted to wring his crazy neck! It was no fair going up against someone with a gun and no sense.

The traffic light was about to change. Any second, the stones under her feet were going to start moving downstream. She hopped her way back to the north side of the street in half the time and sprinted along Broome Street to the east now. A fast left took her zigging up

Mercer. Her breath was coming fast now. The muscles in her legs were starting to ache.

This lower stretch of Mercer was nearly deserted. If she just ran north, she could cut over a couple of blocks and get to the park. She could run her way out of this. She had her Saucony sneakers on her feet. Footsteps sounded behind her, and she accelerated her pace. She knew that if CJ paused to take aim, he'd lose her. *Faster, faster,* she urged her protesting leg muscles.

"You're dead!" he shouted after her.

Not yet, she promised herself. She could see the lights of Houston Street. She was getting close.

Suddenly her escape route was obscured by a `large, silhouetted figure.` As she got closer she realized his presence wasn't coincidental. In the side wash of a streetlight she recognized the face. She didn't know his name, but she'd often seen him with CJ and Marco and the other thugs in the park. A blade winked in his hand.

Ka-ping! CJ fired a shot, which bounced off the cobblestones several feet away.

Oh, this sucked. `This really sucked.` Another wave of adrenaline flowed through her limbs and sizzled in her chest. She dragged in as much air as her lungs could take.

She juked, but he wouldn't let her pass. CJ was hard on her heels, so she couldn't think of stopping. CJ would succeed in shooting her in the back if she gave him any time at all. The space between CJ and his accomplice was closing fast.

Come on. Come on. Come on.

The guy in front of her raised the blade. Gaia didn't stop running. She lifted her arm, drew it back, and without losing a step punched him as hard as she could in the middle of his face. "Sorry," she murmured to him. Judging from the sting in her fist, she'd broken a tooth or two.

A bullet seared past her right shoulder. Another past her knee. The toe of her trusty sneaker caught in a deep groove between the cobblestones and she went down hard, scraping the skin of her forearms and shins.

Shit. Oh, shit.

Her mind was dreamlike again. She didn't feel any pain from her ragged, bleeding skin or from the impact to her wrist and knees. There wasn't anything wrong with her nervous system. It was that every cell of her body was fiercely anticipating the dreaded shot. Some atavistic impulse caused her to bring her hands over her head and curl her knees up in the fetal position.

Time slowed to an eerie, inexplicable stop. Although CJ had been within a few yards of her, the shot didn't come. She took big gulps of air. There were no footsteps. No bullets. She heard nothing.

Slowly, slowly, in disbelief she lifted her head from the street. She turned around cautiously. Her legs shook as she straightened them under the weight of her body.

She peered into the dark, desolate street.

He wasn't there. He really wasn't. `CJ had disappeared`, just when his duck had finally sat.

It was impossible. It made no sense to Gaia. Something told her there was no reasonable explanation for this. But she also knew it would be a mistake to hang around and try to figure out why.

Sometimes I worry

there's something wrong with me. Sometimes I worry I don't actually feel things like regular people do. Often I'm watching the world rather than actually living in it. It's not just that I feel distant from the world. The thing that worries me is that a lot of times, I feel distant from myself. I watch myself like I'd watch an actor in a movie. I think, I observe, I process, but I don't *feel* anything.

Have you ever felt that way? Have you ever sat at the funeral of your great-aunt, for example, and worn a solemn expression on your face and tried to tell yourself all the ways in which it was sad, without actually feeling sad at all?

Have you ever met somebody who said, "Oh my God, that's so funny!" all the time, but never actually laughed? I'm worried that's me.

When my parents split up when

I was in fifth grade, I said all of the things a sad kid says in that circumstance. I even wrung out a few tears. When they got back together ten months later, I shared in the happiness. But for me it was abstract. I could sort of talk myself into feeling something—or at least into believing I felt something—but it didn't come naturally. The emotions certainly didn't rush over me like a wave. I was their eager host, never their victim.

Maybe that's really lucky; I don't know.

But the flip side of experiencing pain abstractly is that you experience pleasure that way, too. Sometimes Heather and I will be eating a romantic dinner together or making out in the park, and it feels really good and everything, but I find myself wondering if I'm missing out on something.

I think this is the reason I can't get over Gaia Moore. I

think it's the reason why I'm intensely attracted to her and repelled by her at the same time. When I'm with her—when I even think of her—I feel things. I feel a wave brewing just out of reach, building and swelling into a breaker of dangerous proportions.

So maybe you can see why I have mixed feelings about getting close to Gaia. I'm not sure I want to lose control. I mean, who would willingly turn himself into a victim?

Maybe that's what love is—I don't know.

Sam couldn't
help smiling.
"Yeah, I'm
getting **hazards**
lucky.
Very lucky."

GAIA IS IN DANGER.

Tom Moore looked up from his laptop computer. He'd been thinking vaguely of Gaia all evening—there was nothing unusual in that—but this was the first time a specific thought coalesced in his mind.

For most of his life he'd discounted notions of telepathy with a certain scorn, but his last five years in the CIA had opened him up to almost any possibility. Was Gaia truly in danger? He felt the familiar worry roiling his stomach.

He looked out the window of the airplane. The plane was either crossing desert or ocean because the sky was almost clear of cloud cover and beneath him was blackness. There wasn't a single light or other sign of human life. He felt terribly lonely.

He wasn't worried about danger in any ordinary sense. Gaia could get herself out of most situations. Tom, of all people, would know. He was the one who'd taught her. In the case of a mugger or purse snatcher going up against Gaia, Tom would frankly fear more for the criminal than her. Gaia was intensely strong, a master of martial arts and most commonly used weapons, and moreover she was free of the fear that compromised ordinary people. Or at least she *was*—

Was.

What did he know of her now?

He knew where she lived and where she went to school. Twice a year he received a heavily encrypted notice of her safety and general progress from the agency. He looked forward to those updates with the fervor of a man grasping for a lifeline, even though they were absurdly short, stiff, and uninformative.

That was it. He knew nothing of her friends, her habits, her pleasures, her emotional state. He had no idea how she was coping with her losses or how close the danger was.

"Sir?" An attendant offered him dinner on a tray. The smell further distressed his stomach. The food on U.S. military planes was even worse than on commercial flights.

"No. Thanks. Maybe later."

"We should be landing in Tel Aviv in approximately seventeen minutes, sir."

"Very well."

Tom looked back at his computer screen. His current briefing involved hundreds and hundreds of pages that had been downloaded via satellite during the course of the flight. One couldn't escape even for a matter of minutes anymore.

He couldn't give his mind to the intricacies of desert diplomacy right now.

There were other dangers to Gaia. More insidious ones that struck close to home. And how could he possibly protect her? Apart from his memories, that was the worst pain he faced.

In the old days, when Gaia was still a child, he'd been purely blown away by her abilities. She was a miracle. His greatest gift. Her brilliance, her beauty, her athleticism, and most of all her God-given sense of honor astonished him every single hour he spent with her. He couldn't imagine what he had done in this life to deserve such a child.

But in these strange days he found himself wishing and praying that his darling, magnificent Gaia were a meek, ordinary creature, likely to catch the attention of no one. A daughter he could trust, above all, to stay out of trouble.

"MAN, WHAT HAPPENED TO YOUR

A Threat

teeth?" Tarick asked. His eyes were bugged out the way they got when he was excited about something.

Marty put his hand over his mouth. He was embarrassed. One front tooth was gone, and the smaller one to the side of it was cracked down the middle. "The girl got in a lucky punch."

CJ snorted and leaned back against the fountain in Washington Square. "The girl laid him out for like five minutes," he explained. "The girl kicked his ass." He was relieved that Gaia had busted somebody else for once.

Tarick turned cold eyes on him. He got up off the fountain wall and paced. "And you, my man. Not having a lot of luck, either?"

CJ could feel his face fall. He'd been dreading this little talk with Tarick for a good reason. "She's tough, man. She's, like, supernatural. And now she's got somebody watching her back. I had a bead on her down on Mercer Street. I had her, I'm telling you, and somebody wearing a parka and a ski mask bagged me from behind and ran off."

"Who was it?" Tarick asked. He looked doubtful.

"Somebody. I don't know. I told you—I couldn't see a face," CJ said.

"You're getting real creative about coming up with excuses," Tarick said.

CJ glared at him. It was unfair. "I am totally serious, man. Marty woulda seen 'em, too, but he was out cold."

Marty looked hurt, but he didn't say anything.

Tarick shook his head. He looked at his watch. He sighed, like he was holding back his temper.

CJ was starting to feel really uneasy. The midday sun had disappeared, and clouds were rolling in from the west. The October air was suddenly cold against CJ's bare head. He felt goose bumps rising all along his back, coursing up his neck and scalp.

"CJ, my man," Tarick started slowly. "This is not hard. You got a powerful weapon. You know where this girl lives. You gotta do what you said you were gonna do."

CJ nodded.

"And you gotta do it, like I said, by midnight Saturday. We're not fooling around here, are we?"

CJ shook his head.

Tarick sat back on the fountain wall just inches away. He put a hand on CJ's bald scalp. "I need to be able to tell the boys we avenged Marco, you know what I mean?"

CJ wished Tarick would remove his hand. It wasn't supposed to be comforting. It was a threat.

"Yeah," CJ mumbled.

"So let's make it crystal clear here, okay?" Tarick increased the pressure of his palm against CJ's shrinking scalp. "Saturday at midnight. If Gaia's not dead . . ."

Tarick paused, and CJ stared at him expectantly.

"Then you are."

SEARCH: THOMAS MOORE

No Match Found

Search: Special Agent Moore

Search

```
Arlington, Virginia
No Match Found

Search: Federal Agent #4466
No Match Found

Search: Michael Sage
No Match Found

Search: Robert W. Connelly
No Match Found

Search: Enigma
No Match Found

Search: My goddamned father, you
stupid morons.
No Match Found

Search:
```

Gaia threw the mouse at the monitor. She was getting frustrated. She'd hacked her way into the files of the appropriate federal agency, but the search engine refused to recognize her father's name, his old badge number, or any of his old aliases.

Was he with the agency anymore? Was he even still alive?

She'd always told herself the government would notify her if he were dead. The agency was the only place that knew her whereabouts. She'd also told herself that her dad had to have been up to some pretty covert and important stuff—like single-handedly saving the planet, for instance—to have abandoned her this way.

She told herself these things, but that didn't make them true.

Gaia heard a noise. Oh, no. If Ella was home, she'd have to jump out the window again. A moment spent with that woman was like `chewing tinfoil`. And this was not Gaia's computer to be performing illegal operations—or actually any operations—on.

She crept to the door of George's office on silent feet. The house was still. She crept back to the computer. According to the time in the right corner of the screen, she had seven minutes before Ella was due home. George wouldn't be home till after seven.

Okay. Now what? She drummed her fingers on the mouse pad. She didn't know the name her father used. She didn't know where he lived. She didn't know where he was working. He'd never, in almost five years, made any attempt to contact her. Not quite your doting father.

She felt the old anger building. Time for a little distraction. As far as Gaia was concerned, a little distraction was worth a lot of solution.

Okay. Plan 2. Sam. She had been less successful with plan 2 than plan 1, if that was possible. Could you get lower than zero? Was it appropriate to bring in negative numbers for the sake of comparison?

She aimed her fingers back at the keyboard. She called up an address-locator web site and typed in Sam's basic information.

Aha! All was not lost! Within seconds she had a definitive answer:

SamMoon3@culdesac.com

She was just one (borrowed) computer away from direct and private conversation with Sam.

Ha!

And she'd done it while leaving one full minute to hide before Ella got home.

SAM LAY IN HIS LUMPY, STEEL-

Getting Lucky

frame twin bed, considering Heather's note. He didn't need to look at the note to consider it because he had stared at it so long, he'd committed it to memory.

Heather was ready. How long had he wanted to hear those

words? How long had he fantasized about this very thing?

God, and after seeing him with Gaia, he'd expected her to be pissed or at least suspicious. But she wasn't. She was angelic and totally trusting. And he was an undeserving bastard who was about to get unbe-lievably lucky. Almost too lucky to be true.

So what was the problem?

Forget it. There wasn't a problem. He wasn't going to get derailed by thinking about the problem.

If there was a problem, that is. Which there wasn't.

He was really, really happy as hell, even if he didn't realize it one hundred percent yet.

Time to think about Saturday night. That was only two days away. Heather was coming here, to his dorm room, and they were going to . . .

Oh, man. He was starting to feel tingly. He stared up at the stained acoustical tile on the ceiling. It wasn't the most romantic sight. He glanced at the piles of clothes around his room. He looked at the mound of chess books, magazines, and clippings blanketing his desk. He eyed the new box of syringes he'd just bought for his diabetes treatments. He propped himself up on his elbow and studied the grayish sheet covering his mattress. Exactly when was the last time he'd washed that sheet? Had it been gray to start out with, or was it born white? The fact that he couldn't remember the an-swer to either question wasn't a good sign.

Wait a minute. Heather. Gorgeous, perfectly dressed, sweet-smelling Heather was going to come into this room? This pigpen? This landfill? Was he seriously thinking of lying her down on this filthy bed? It wasn't only unromantic; it was probably a health hazard.

He sat up with a jolt and swung his legs off the bed. He swept up a pile of clothes and threw them on the bed beside him. Lurking under the pile were dust creatures that belonged in a horror movie. Thank God his mother couldn't see this.

In his freshman year he'd kept up some semblance of hygiene (if you defined the term very loosely) because he had a roommate. But this year he had his own minuscule room, attached to a common room shared by three other guys. He pretended to get indignant when the other guys left spilled beer on the vomit-colored carpet in the common room or ground Cheetos into microscopic orange dust underfoot. But that didn't mean he'd spent even one second looking after his own room. Usually if Heather came around, they hung out in the common room and watched TV or raided the minifridge. She hadn't inspected the frightening cave where he slept.

It was high time to reacquaint himself with the laundry room in the basement. He'd sweep out whatever flora and fauna were growing under his bed. He'd get rid of the altar to Gary Kasparov—no need to subject Heather to a full-on dork fest. Besides, the knitted brow of Kasparov didn't exactly put you in the mood.

He was just consolidating his massive clothes pile when the door swung open.

"Hey, Moon."

It was Mike Suarez, one of his suite mates.

"Does the word *knock* mean anything to you, Suarez?" Sam asked.

"Does the phrase 'lock your friggin' door if you don't want company' mean anything to you?"

Sam laughed. "The lock is busted. Half the time you turn the knob, it falls off into your hand." He made a mental note to get that fixed before Saturday.

Suarez watched him clean for a minute.

"You planning on getting lucky?"

Sam paused and rubbed his nose. Dust bits were flying in his nostrils, making them itch. "What do you mean?"

"I can think of only one reason why a guy cleans his room," Suarez said suggestively.

Sam's energy sagged at the thought of being such a cliché. He tossed the ball of laundry on the ground.

"So?"

Sam couldn't help smiling. "Yeah, I'm getting lucky. Very lucky."

Can He Resist?

"SHE FOUND NOTHING, OF COURSE," Ella stated, her voice ringing shrilly through the wide-open loft space, bouncing around its few polished surfaces.

"I see. And you were there watching her for the duration of her search?"

Ella's face showed impatience. "Certainly."

He pressed his lips together to signal his own waning patience. Ella, with her sleek body, her colorfully revealing clothing, and her poorly concealed moodiness acted as much the angry teenager as his bewitching Gaia. But as potently as Ella annoyed him, she had a value far beyond the dog-loyal bodyguards who remained within fifteen feet of him at all times. "Did she display any knowledge of her father's whereabouts?"

"No. Nothing current."

He flicked a tiny piece of lint from his dark blue slacks. "I see." He sipped coffee. "And he has made no attempt to contact her?" The question was rhetorical. He didn't even know why he'd asked it.

"No," Ella confirmed.

"How can he resist?" he mused in a quiet voice, mostly to himself.

"Sir?"

"How can he resist making contact with Gaia?

She's all he has in the world after what happened to Katia. He adores her. He needs her. He knows she's bound to get into trouble." He was really talking only to himself.

"Yes, sir. Would you like me to continue to keep a record of her computer activity in case she makes any strides toward finding him?" Ella asked. Even when her words were perfectly dutiful, her tone was `petulant`.

He made a sharp exhale through his nose, which was the closest he came to amusement. "She won't find him. Although I despise Tom, I can't pretend he's an idiot, can I? She'll never find him, although you're welcome to leave a few red herrings that will keep her busy trying. I'm banking on the belief—no, the knowledge—that Tom will find *her.*"

He picked up the impossibly slender computer from the table beside him. He'd just had a very simple and appealing idea. He sat back and crossed his legs, the computer perched on his knee. "Tom will come for her, and when he does, he's mine."

There's one thing I want more than anything else, and I know I can never have it. I don't mean Sam or finding my dad. I'm talking about something inside myself.

I want to be brave.

And I'm not brave, in case you're wondering. Maybe I could have been brave, but I guess I'll never know.

The reason is that you can't separate bravery from fear. This is something I've thought about a lot. The people with the most fear have the greatest opportunity to be brave. A woman who is terrified of the water would be braver sticking her big toe in the swimming pool than I would be surfing a thirty-foot breaker in the Pacific Ocean. She would be overcoming something. She would be challenging herself. She would experience the pleasure of expanding her world, the freedom of exercising her will. I would be surfing a wave.

My mom used to say that a poor person who gave a dime to charity was more generous than a rich one who gave hundreds of dollars. In this example, I would be Bill Gates. Only richer.

I know for a fact that my mother was claustrophobic. And most especially, she was afraid of tunnels. Deeply, seriously afraid. I think it had something to do with her childhood in Russia, which was pretty tough. Anyway, the reason I know is because when I was seven, all my friends were taking gymnastics class a few miles away and I was desperate to go. My mom didn't want to take me at first, but I begged and pleaded. I wouldn't shut up about it. Finally my mom agreed. It turned out you had to go through a tunnel to get there. So even though I wasn't a very sensitive or nice kid, I realized my mom was basically flipping out in that tunnel. Her hands were dripping wet on the steering wheel, and her skin was whitish gray. She made these weird little moaning sounds. When we finally got out of the tunnel, she pulled over on the shoulder, rested her head on the steering wheel, and just stayed like that. I was upset, but she held me and promised me everything was fine.

Every Saturday for almost two years after that, my mother drove me to gymnastics and picked me up.

When I think of that, I'm filled with horrible, wrenching, miserable guilt. I wish so much I would have dropped that stupid gymnastics class and never gone back. But I didn't. And I can't change the past.

So instead of that, I wish that for one single moment in my life, I could be brave like my mom.

Sam's long, **fragile**
beautiful
body **under-**
claimed
all of **standing**
her senses.

DEAR SAM,

I have a very strange favor to ask you. I know you don't know me that well, and what you know of me you probably don't like. I am really, truly, sincerely sorry for what happened to Heather in the park and for the part I played in it. I know she's your girlfriend, so what I'm about to ask will sound particularly insane, but

Sent Mail

Dear Sam,

There's this guy named CJ, a friend and fellow neo-Nazi of Marco's, the guy who tried to kill us after slashing Zolov in the park. Well, would you believe Marco is dead and CJ thinks I did it? CJ has completely lost his mind and is now hell-bent on killing me. And I came to this realization that before I die, I really want to

Dear Sam,

I know I must seem like trouble to you. I know it must seem like bad luck follows me around. I know you probably wish you'd never seen my face, which I

can totally understand. And lucky for
you, after this coming weekend you'll
most likely never have to see me again.
But before then, I was wondering if you
wouldn't mind

Dear Sam,
   I am confessing to you in total confidence that in my seventeen years,
I've had very little romantic experience. Okay, none. Well, actually there
was this kid in seventh grade who kind
of liked me but—
   Anyway, I've been thinking about you
a lot recently, and I was wondering
whether—

Dear Sam,
   Will you have sex with me? Saturday
night, no questions, no commitment.

Oh, shit. Ella was home. Gaia had to get out of
George's office right away. Ella would lose it if she
found Gaia in here and there was no way Gaia wanted
to deal with the witch in her present state of mind.
   Oh. Oh. Gaia's eyes flew over the computer monitor.
What should she do? Should she save one of these horrible letters to finish later? She had so many windows

open on the screen, she couldn't keep track of them. She heard Ella's heels clicking down the hallway. Oh, no. Um. Um.

In desperation she clicked on the Send Later icon. She clicked the X in the top-right corner to exit the on-line service. Ella was slowing down. She was right outside!

Gaia threw herself under George's desk and held her breath.

Ella paused in the open office doorway.

Don't come in here! Gaia commanded silently. *Go away* now!

Ella paid no heed to the telepathic messages. She walked right up to the computer and stared, squinting, at the screen.

Gaia knew for a fact that Ella was seriously nearsighted. But the woman was too vain to wear glasses and too stupid to put in contacts.

Ella placed her hand on the mouse.

What could she possibly want with the computer? Gaia wondered. No interface was user-friendly enough for Ella. Gaia had often snickered at the full library of "Such and Such for Dummies" titles on Ella's bookshelf.

Ella continued to stare dumbly at the screen. Her feet were a matter of inches from Gaia's shins. *Don't look down,* Gaia ordered in her head. *Do* not! Gaia tried to make her body as absolutely small as possible.

Ella clicked the mouse. Gaia heard the modem dialing up the on-line service and, within a few seconds, connecting. "Hello," the synthesized computer voice chirped.

What was going on? Gaia had never seen Ella in the same room with a computer before. Had she suddenly discovered the joy of on-line sex? Had somebody told her about the Victoria's Secret web site?

Ella squinted at the screen for another moment and clicked the mouse again.

Please don't be long, Gaia begged silently. Her knees hurt, and her back was cramping. It was so dusty under George's desk, she felt a sneeze threatening. If Ella was going shopping, it could take hours.

Then, as though obeying silent orders, Ella stood up, turned around and walked away. She walked right back down the hallway and up the creaky stairs.

Gaia's heart soared with relief. She uncrumpled her limbs and climbed out from under the desk. She was so busy congratulating herself, she didn't bother to look at the screen at first. Then the blinking box caught the corner of her eye. She came closer to read it.

"Your mail was sent."

A shiver crept down Gaia's spine. What? What mail had been sent? Probably just something of Ella's, Gaia tried to comfort herself.

She clicked on the file icon to investigate. Then she

clicked the Mail Sent icon. She was starting to get a very bad feeling in her stomach.

It was one of Gaia's files. Somehow, by going online, Ella had sent a Send Later file. But which one? Gaia clicked twice on the file.

It came up instantly, the letters twice as big and black as any others on the screen. She felt like someone had kicked her brutally hard in the middle of her chest.

Dear Sam,

Will you have sex with me? Saturday night, no questions, no commitment.

TOM MOORE WAS CROSSING ANOTHER

endless desert. For a man who traveled tens of thousands of miles every week of his life, he certainly spent a great deal of time in the same chair, studying the same screen. For a man who hadn't seen his daughter in five

years, he certainly spent a great deal of time thinking about her.

Hundreds, thousands of pages of briefings swam

before his eyes. He closed the document and looked around him. He was so accustomed to the hum of jet engines, he could hardly sleep without it. The only other passenger, his personal assistant, was asleep.

The ever present satellite connection allowed him to get on-line. He'd promised himself he wouldn't do this, but tonight, well, tonight his mind was once again burning with worry for Gaia, and he couldn't ignore it any longer.

His first search for her name called up nothing. That was as it should be if the U.S. government was doing what they'd promised. Then he reduced the search to just her first name and conducted it globally, typing in a series of passwords that allowed him a degree of access allowed to only a handful of people— access to virtually all e-mail posted on the web, for example. This turned up an enormous list. He allowed himself a look into one file. Just one. He'd pick it wisely, then he'd stop this nonsense and get back to his work.

He scrolled through the upper part of the list. He stopped on a note tagged by the re: field. It read:

re: supergaia

He opened the file:

To: jackboot
From: stika

Gaia sighting at WSW. Call set for
2100 Sat. 2 guys and metal.

It was an unfortunately good guess. Tom's worry intensified as he read easily between the lines. He felt distressingly sure this Gaia was his Gaia. He could see that the posting had come from the New York City area and could easily assume that WSW meant Washington Square West, a very short distance from George's home and the school Gaia attended.

Now that he'd opened Pandora's box, the ghosts were all around him. He'd known this could happen. Now it didn't matter how critically his presence was needed in Beirut. He pressed the button for the intercom that connected his voice to the cockpit.

"Gentlemen," he said calmly, "I'm afraid I need to order a change in destination. Let's touch down for refueling. We'll be crossing the Atlantic tonight."

GAIA PADDED QUIETLY DOWN THE

darkened hallway. She'd never been in a college dormitory before. When she reached the room number she'd gotten from the student directory, she paused. She combed

Urgent Longing

her fingers through her hair, pushing long strands back from her face. She pulled self-consciously at the hem of her exquisitely soft red velvet tank dress. Taking a breath, she turned the heavy brass knob and swung open the door.

Her breath caught. He was there. He lay on his bed, his strong arms folded behind his head, propping his upper body against the bed frame. The rest of the room was oddly indistinct, shadowy and blurred. Sam's long, beautiful body claimed all of her senses.

He looked at her. He wasn't surprised. He wasn't upset. He wasn't happy, exactly, either. He looked . . . serious. Had he known she would come now? Had he wanted it?

His feet were bare and crossed at the ankles. His loose gray sweatpants were turned up a few times at the bottom. Keeping his eyes on her face, he swung his knees over the side of the small bed and stood. He started toward her, then stopped, leaving two feet between them. Slowly he reached his arm, making a bridge across the air, and placed two fingers on the inside of her elbow, that vulnerable place where oxygen-thirsty blood coursed closest to her surface. A chill stole up her neck and dispersed over her scalp.

She'd come prepared with a storm of explanations in her head: (1)Why. (2)Why now. (3) Why him. But in this moment, stating them felt like it would break the tentative, fragile understanding, nurtured and protected by silence.

She took a step closer. This was hard for her. She bent her elbow and wrapped her fingers around his wrist. Was he pulling her, or was she pulling him? She wasn't sure. All she knew was that she was now close enough to feel the warmth radiating from his skin. He put his arms around her. She felt his fingers on the nape of her neck. Suddenly her arms were circling his taut waist, pressing him against her, crushing her breasts against his broad chest.

God, she was dizzy. She was light-headed, giddy, tingling with excitement and disbelief. Her heart was too full to stay in her rib cage. Tears gathered under her lashes.

He bent his head down so close to hers, she could feel his soft breath on her cheek. Oh God, how she wanted this kiss. She'd waited a lifetime for it. She breathed in his subtle, masculine smell and faint mixture of clean sweat and eucalyptus-scented shaving cream. She lifted her mouth to his.

Her mind was a tumultuous sea, with thoughts listing and bobbing there. And all at once an image arrived. It was an image of her body, scarred and wounded, becoming whole and perfect under his healing lips. The picture was beautiful, and she wished she could keep it, but a wave crashed through, sending thoughts spinning and surfing in the chop.

Please, kiss me, she found herself wishing. *Please. I need you.*

And then, in a cruel trick played by fate, Sam not only failed to kiss her; he dissolved completely. He vanished into air. He was replaced by dim, grayish sunlight, a tangle of mismatched covers. The magical night in his bed was replaced by a harsh, wrenching morning in hers. No, not even in hers. In one that belonged to George and Ella. Her velvet dress was replaced by a worn-out T-shirt from Jerry's Crab House.

She turned over and buried her head in her pillow. Tears stung in her eyes. The loneliness was almost unbearable. As reality spread out before her, its stark contrast to the dream made it that much harder to take.

She wanted so much to retrieve the feelings . . . and that image.

What was that image again?

In that first moment of waking, it teased her with its closeness. It danced and sparkled on a wavelet at her feet. But then the vast ocean pulled back the tide into its dark, infinite belly, and now Gaia was faced with the terror of never finding it again. If she could only find it, she felt sure it would give her strength and maybe hope.

But she was left with nothing but the taste of Sam—her fantasy of Sam—on her lips and an urgent, painful longing in her heart.

You may have noticed my name sounds familiar. I share it with a number of people, but most importantly the great scholar, statesman, and saint Sir Thomas More, born in England in 1478.

My mother was a devout Roman Catholic, and I assumed she picked the name to remind me of piety above all else. To remind me to choose God-given principles over king or scholarship or art . . . or even family.

Since I was a child, I felt the pressure of this name. I took it seriously. That's the kind of person I am, I suppose. I wanted to serve my country. I wanted to serve God. And if sacrifices were called for, I wanted to possess the courage to make them with honor.

My namesake set forth an almost impossible record of bravery. He watched his father imprisoned by King Henry VII because of his own deeds. He wrote a brilliant critique of English

(SIR) THOMAS MORE

society in his work <u>Utopia.</u>
Ultimately he was canonized for
putting his head on the chopping
block rather than compromising
his basic beliefs for the benefit
of King Henry VIII.

I never questioned the right-
ness of More's example until
after I lost Katia and then Gaia.
Now the question haunts me every
day of my life.

In an ironic and unfortunate
twist of fate, not long after my
mother's death, I read a letter
she'd written to her father
around the time I was born. In it
I discovered she didn't name me
after Thomas More, honored saint
and statesman. She named me after
Thomas Moore, the Irish romantic
poet.

But maybe
he would be
curious. **about**
And maybe a
tiny bit **sex**
interested?
Was it
possible?

"GAIA MOORE? ARE YOU WITH US?"

Gaia snapped her head up. She glanced around at the unsympathetic faces of her classmates. Which class was this? What were they talking about? She gave her head a shake to dislodge her heavy, demanding preoccupations.

A Creepy Pervert

Let's see. Ummmm. Ms. Rupert. That would be history. European history. Which century were they in now? Which country? She hadn't looked at her textbook in a while.

"No, ma'am, I'm not," Gaia replied truthfully.

Ms. Rupert's eyes bulged with annoyance. "You're not, are you? Then would you be so kind as to share with me and the rest of the class what you find so much more captivating than the court of King Henry VIII?"

Gaia drummed her fingers on her desk. Did Ms. Rupert *really* want to know the answer to that question?

"Yes, Gaia? I'm waiting." Her hands were on her hips in a caricature of impatience.

Apparently she did. "I was thinking about sex, ma'am. I was thinking about having sex," Gaia stated.

The class disintegrated into laughter and whispering.

Everybody was staring at Gaia. It wasn't nice laughter. Since the incident with Heather getting slashed in the park, Gaia wasn't exactly Miss Popularity. She shrugged.

Ms. Rupert looked like she'd swallowed her tongue. She spluttered and turned deep crimson before she could get a word out. "G-Gaia Moore, get out of my class! Go to the principal's office *now!*"

"Yes, ma'am," Gaia said agreeably, striding to the door.

This was a lucky break, she thought, walking down the deserted hall with lightness in her step. The vice principal would keep her waiting outside his office for ages as a phony display of his importance and full-to-bursting schedule, and it was much easier to obsess about Sam without Ms. Rupert droning on about Henry VIII and all the various people's heads he'd chopped off.

What was Sam thinking? That was the central question nagging her. Assuming he'd received her psychotic e-mail and could tell it was from her, what must he be thinking?

That she was a nympho, for one thing. That she gave new meaning to the word *desperate,* for another. That she was an opportunistic couple wrecker, for a third.

But maybe he would be curious. And maybe a tiny bit interested? Was it possible?

She hardly dared hope.

In some ways she was happy she'd gotten the ball rolling, even if the note did make her seem like someone who deserved to be arrested and put under a restraining order. At least she'd opened up the conversation. At least it would give her the opportunity to say, Hey, Sam, I know this is weird, I know I seem like a complete sex-starved lunatic, but can I just explain?

She ascended a flight of stairs and was just passing the computer lab when she stopped. Hmmm. The room was dark, empty, and filled, not surprisingly, with computers. She needed only one, and she needed it only for a minute or two. Ms. Rupert would eat her own arm if she knew Gaia was making a detour, but so what?

Gaia crept to the back corner of the room and revived the sleeping monitor. Quickly she located the Internet server and signed on. She went to the site where she kept a mailbox and typed in her password.

Oh, God. There was mail! She held her breath and clicked on the envelope symbol. Her heart leaped. It was from Sam Moon! He had replied!

Was this good? Was this bad? At least it was something.

Now, calm down, she commanded herself. Okay. She clicked on the letter to open it.

Dear Gaia13,

Your letter was an unbelievable turn-
on. I've been hard since I read it. You
name the time and place and I am there,
honey. I am all over you. I will make
you scream, baby. I will make you beg
for more. Once you feel my—

Gaia swallowed. She couldn't read any more. Her
stomach felt queasy. This wasn't what she . . . she
couldn't quite believe he...

Her eye caught on something in the routing information at the bottom of the letter. A phrase of coded
gobbledygook in which she picked out the word
Canada. She clicked on another series of boxes to get
Sam Moon's personal profile.

Name: Sam Moon
Home: Victoria, BC
Age: 62

Gaia's body was flooded with relief. She almost had
to laugh. She had blatantly propositioned a sixty-two-
year-old Canadian man. She exited the program and
turned off the computer.

On the bright side, her beloved Sam Moon wasn't a
creepy pervert, although he shared his name with one.
On the less bright side, she was back to square one.

"SO *WHAT* IS THE PROBLEM?" DANNY

How He Feels

Bell wanted to know. He said it so loudly, Sam had to hold the phone a few inches from his ear.

"Well, I guess . . . I don't know." Sam scratched the back of his scalp absently. "I'm not really sure how I feel about her."

Sam watched colorful pipes weaving three-dimensionally through the computer screen that sat on his crowded dorm-room desk. He'd set the screen saver to come on after ten minutes of idleness, but when he was talking on the phone or procrastinating, the damn pipes seemed to take over his screen every thirty seconds.

"You're not sure how you *feel* about her?" Danny didn't go far out of his way to hide the incredulity in his voice. "Let me get this straight. You have a stupendously gorgeous girlfriend who you've been with for six months. She wants to have sex, and you're suddenly not sure how you *feel?*"

Sam could picture exactly the look on Danny's face, even though he was three thousand miles away. Danny was his oldest and closest friend from the neighborhood in Maryland where he grew up. In fact, Danny was the only friend he had from the old days, before Sam had remade himself from a stammering, buck-toothed chess nerd into a decently dressed, mainstream guy who went out with beautiful girls and cared what other people thought.

It was funny. Sam had changed, but Danny hadn't. Danny was still an unapologetic lover of chess and Myst and Star Wars. He was an engineering student at Stanford University, which was probably what Sam would have been had he stayed the course.

"Okay, there's a little more to it than that," Sam confessed. "See, I met this other girl."

"Aha," Danny said in a know-it-all way. "I had a feeling there was something more here. So what happened? Did you go out with her behind Heather's back?"

The pipes were hypnotic. "No, not exactly."

"But you're attracted to her."

Sam let out a groan. "Yeah, you could say that."

"What's she like?"

"Well . . . she's different from any girl I've ever met," Sam began slowly. "She's an uncanny chess player, for one thing. She's probably at my level or close to it."

Danny was silent for at least thirty seconds. "No way," he said at last.

"I'm serious."

"Jesus. What's her name? Have I heard of her or read about her?"

"No. She's mysterious like that," Sam explained. "She hasn't come up through the normal chess ranks.

I don't know anybody who's played her in competition. I don't know how she learned. She's just . . . brilliant."

"Are you sure you're not just stupid when you're around her?" Danny asked.

Sam laughed. "I *am* stupid when I'm around her. But she really is good. The other guys who play chess in the park worship her—and not for her body, either. I wouldn't even play her again 'cause she'd probably beat me in a matter of seconds."

Danny was struck to the point of speechlessness. "So, what else do you know about her?" he asked finally.

"Well, I guess her parents aren't around anymore, and from what I can tell, she has very few if any friends. She just moved to New York, but I don't know from where."

"That's awful. Did you ask her where she came from?" Danny asked.

"No." The pipes were now making Sam nauseous. He moved from his desk chair and paced the three available feet of space in the room. One of the few benefits of a minuscule room was that the ancient phone cord reached every corner of it. "I can't explain why, exactly. It's like . . . I don't know. She doesn't give you the feeling that she really welcomes questions. She seems kind of . . . haunted in a way. I guess she's been through a lot in her life. I had this weird reaction to her the first time I saw her, like I knew everything about her even though I didn't know anything. I was intensely attracted to her and sort of scared off at the same time."

Sam heard Mike Suarez and one of his other suite mates, Brendon Moss, firing up the TV for a baseball game. He moved to close the door to his room.

One of the great things about Danny was that he wasn't cool. He wasn't jaded or sarcastic. He wasn't embarrassed about having a real conversation. Sam could tell Danny things he wouldn't consider telling his other friends.

"Does that make any sense?" Sam finished.

"Um. Not really," Danny answered.

Sam sat down on his bed. (Now covered with a clean, nearly white sheet.) "Yeah, I know," he said. "I guess I'm hesitant to ask her anything because I'm not all that sure I want to hear the answers."

"Huh," Danny said. "Maybe she's a spy. Or an alien. Did you ever see that movie *Species*?"

Sam laughed again.

"So what does this girl look like?" Danny asked. "She can't be as pretty as Heather."

Sam thought that one over for a minute. "In a way she's not, and in a way she's much, much more beautiful. She doesn't dress like Heather, or wear jewelry, or keep her hair nice. You don't get the feeling she's trying to be pretty. And she's got this kind of hard, angry expression on her face a lot of the time. But if you can get past that and really see her face and her eyes . . . she's by far the most amazing-looking girl I've ever met. I can't explain it."

"Wow," Danny said. "So why don't you try it out with this girl?" he suggested after considering it for a few moments. "It sounds like she's gotten under your skin."

"She has. That's exactly what it is," Sam said, rearranging his long legs as the weary dorm-room bed groaned under his weight. "But first of all, there's Heather to think of. And also, this girl is all about trouble. I can't even begin to explain to you the kind of trouble she causes. Heather is safe, and she's great. And she's . . . ready."

Danny laughed. "Yeah. God, I wish I had your problems."

Sam walked over to the window and looked out at the courtyard. In New York City they called it a courtyard even if it was ten square feet of poured concrete, overfilled with plastic garbage cans and piles of recycling. "It's not as fun as it sounds," Sam said.

"Well, there's one obvious thing to do," Danny pointed out.

"Yeah, what's that?"

"Take out a piece of paper. At the top put Heather's name on one side and the other girl's name on the other, and make a list."

Heather	_Gaia_
My girlfriend	_Not my girlfriend_
My parents love her	_Would frighten my parents_
Not good at chess	_Great at chess_
Belongs in a magazine	_Doesn't_
Safe	_Trouble_
Loves me	_Probably doesn't give a shit_
Ready	_?_

Sam studied his list for a moment, crumpled it in a tight ball, and tossed it in the garbage. What was he, some kind of idiot?

His heart,
his life,
his sense
of life's **ghosts**
possibilities
was shaken.

TOM MOORE KNEW HE WAS CRAZY TO BE doing this. He walked down Waverly Place in the West Village with his head throbbing and his heart full. Just two blocks from here, in a tiny

Remembering Katia

bookshop, he'd first laid eyes on Katia. It was probably the most important moment of his entire life, and yet he hadn't been back here in twenty years.

It was, without question, love at first sight. It was a freezing cold day in February, and the city was bleak and dismal. The previous night's snow was no more than a brown, muddy obstacle between sidewalk and street. He'd been looking for a rare translation of Thucydides for his graduate thesis. He was stewing about something—that his adviser hadn't credited him in a recent publication. He'd seen her as soon as he'd opened the door. The shop was a tiny square, for one thing. But Katia seemed to draw every atom in the place to her. In that moment Tom's entire life evaporated and a new one started.

She was sitting cross-legged in the corner, bent forward with a book on her lap. He remembered she wore gray woolen tights, under battered rubber boots and a red knit dress. Her hair was long, dark, and straight, falling in a shiny column on either side of her face. She was devouring a stack of books the way a starving person would devour a plate of food. He would never forget that image of her.

Up until that point, he'd had many relationships with women. Fellow college and grad students, pretty ones he'd met through friends. He'd traveled with girlfriends, even lived with one for a few months. And yet his heart had never been stirred until the time he saw Katia, a naive nineteen-year-old with cheap, old-fashioned Eastern Bloc clothing and a thick Russian accent. And then it was shaken.

His heart, his life, his sense of life's possibilities was shaken. In her eyes he became somebody he could believe in.

He paused after crossing Seventh Avenue. He shouldn't be here at all. He'd learned in the hardest possible way that a man who'd made enemies like his could not afford to have a family. His disguise was minimal. His presence was needed in Beirut. He could walk straight into Gaia if he wasn't careful. He was drowning his usually sane mind in a riptide of memories.

Still he continued on. And then stopped dead in his tracks. Of course. Of course. Virtually every single thing in New York City had changed in the last twenty years, and that bookstore remained. Katia was gone. The person he'd been with Katia was gone.

Their beautiful daughter, the greatest pleasure in their lives, was alone. And the damn bookstore winked at him smugly. The riptide threatened. It dragged on his feet. Tom walked faster.

If he had any sense, he'd get back on that plane, his home away from work, and resume his mission. It was all he could show for the terrible sacrifices he'd made.

But he couldn't. He needed to see Gaia just once. From afar, of course. He'd drink her in with his thirsty eyes, make sure she was safe, and get back to his work.

Although Thomas, sainted statesman, had boarded the plane back in Tel Aviv, it appeared that the romantic poet had disembarked here in New York.

"WAIT, SO YOU'RE NOT GOING TO

Robbie's tomorrow night?" Melanie asked Heather, scrambling to keep up with her friend's long, efficient strides. "According to Shauna, it's a two kegger with zero parents."

Darts

Heather shook her head. "Nope. Other plans." She smiled in a way that was mysterious and maybe a tiny bit smug. She glanced up the crowded block of Eighth Street. There were two good shoe stores before they even got to Patricia Field, and Melanie and Cory Parkes were already loaded down with shopping bags and struggling to keep up. Heather was famous among her friends for being a very fast walker and an intensely picky shopper, but the truth was, she no longer had a duplicate of her parents' credit card, the way many of her friends did.

"Other plans?" Cory demanded, gulping up the bait as always.

"Sam and I are . . . getting together," Heather offered.

"So bring him to the party," Melanie said, falling back for a moment as she rearranged her bags between her tired hands.

"I promised him we'd be alone for once," Heather explained.

"Oooh. Does this mean you're taking things to the next level?" Cory asked.

Heather smiled ambiguously. "It's a thought."

Melanie was getting that look. Her face crumpled a little when conversation turned to Sam, partly because she was envious that Heather had a mythically desirable boyfriend but also because it got in the way of Melanie's supercontrolling go-girl solidarity. Heather had a pessimistic feeling that Melanie's allegiances would change once she found a guy she thought was worthy.

"Besides," Heather said. "You know I can't drag

him to high school parties anymore." She pulled up short at Broadway Shoes, one of their regular destinations. "Do you want to go here?" she asked.

"Let's go straight to Patricia Field," Melanie said. "They have these really cute mod dresses."

Cory strode alongside Heather eagerly. "Are you going to get the orange skirt with the thingies along the bottom you tried on last time? It looked so, so cool on you."

Heather shrugged. "Maybe. The lining was kind of itchy." The lining was only mildly itchy; the skirt cost ninety-five dollars.

They were a few yards down the block from Ozzie's Cafe when Heather's stomach dropped. It was funny. She saw Ed Fargo most days of her life. It had been over two years since they'd broken up. Yet still her physical reaction on seeing him was always the same—sometimes stronger, sometimes weaker, but always present.

He was sitting in his wheelchair at a front table by the window, seeming to scan every person who passed. His dark hair was crying out to be combed, and his awful midnineties cargo pants belonged in a Dumpster. But Ed managed to be powerfully attractive nonetheless. His jaw was a little sharp and his straight nose was a little long, but he had possibly the most beautiful mouth that had ever graced the face of a man. The parts of his face, though not flawless the way Sam's were, came together in a striking and disarming way.

As often happened, Heather had that strange, sad feeling of disconnect, knowing the ghost of the person she'd loved desperately, the one with legs that worked, was lurking within the person in the ghastly wheelchair, who needed special ramp entrances and kneeling buses.

She was shallow. She knew that. Ed was still the same person inside. He was still the same person inside. No matter how many times she said it and thought it, she couldn't make herself believe it.

She stopped abruptly and rapped on the glass. Ed looked up and smiled. It was a guarded smile. She was in a position to know the difference.

Her friends were already several steps ahead, but they had stopped now and were waiting for her. "Go ahead," she called, waving them on. "I'll meet you there in, like, five minutes." When they paused, she gestured again, less patiently. "Go. I swear I'll be there in a couple of minutes."

Once her friends started walking again, Heather stepped into Ozzie's and was embraced by the thick smell of coffee. "Hey, Ed," she said, sitting down in the empty chair across from him.

"Hey," he said back. "What's going on?"

"Nothing. Just, you know, shopping with the girlfriends."

Ed nodded.

"You're waiting for someone?" Heather asked. Before he had a chance to answer, she said, "Let me guess. Gaia Moore, right?"

He looked uncomfortable. "No, not really."

"Oh, come on."

"What?" Ed said defensively. "Sometimes she comes by here after school and we have coffee. Sometimes I have coffee by myself."

Heather put her index finger on a drop of coffee that had spilled on the table. She spread the liquid in a widening circle. "You guys have gotten to be good friends, it seems like."

"Yeah."

Heather laughed at a memory, pretending it was impulsive. "Did you hear about her classic line in Rupert's class today?"

Though still guarded, Ed now looked interested in spite of himself. "No. What?"

"Rupert asked her why she wasn't paying attention, and Gaia said, and this is an exact quote, 'I was thinking about sex. I was thinking about having sex.'" Heather laughed again. "What a freak. People were mimicking her all afternoon. I'm surprised you missed it."

Ed waited for her to finish without even a smile. What had happened to the guy's sense of humor?

Heather needed a way in. She needed to make Ed

talk to her. She sat back in her chair and rolled a piece of her hair between her finger and thumb.

"I've heard Gaia's stoking a major crush," she said, tossing a dart into the winds.

Ed remained wary. "Oh, yeah?"

"So says the rumor mill," Heather said provocatively. She took a calculated risk with a second dart. "Word is, the crush is on you. Tannie got a look at her notebook in precal. . . ."

Bull's-eye. Ed's cheeks flushed. He met her eyes with poorly masked excitement and curiosity.

On the one hand, Heather was pleased that her instincts served her so well. On the other hand, it pissed her off that Ed was obviously falling victim to Gaia, too. Had Gaia Moore been put on earth to punish her?

Ed crumpled an empty sugar packet tightly between his fingers. "I don't know about that," he mumbled. Guarded as he was, he did want to talk. "I think it's more about sex."

Heather yawned. Once she got started, it was genuine. "What do you mean?"

"Oh, I don't know." Ed seemed to wave a thought away. "She wants to lose her virginity. I guess if she's telling Ms. Rupert's class about it, it's not a big secret."

Heather looked in her purse, ostensibly for lip balm. "And who's the lucky guy?" she said suggestively.

"She hasn't said. It's a mystery."

"Aha." In near perfect detail, Heather's mind called up the image of Gaia and Sam sitting together on that bench in the park. Heather was starting to get an unpleasant feeling about this.

Heather located the tube of Chap Stick and ran it over her lips. "It's not a mystery to me," she said confidently.

"What do you mean?" Ed asked tentatively, crushing the bit of paper in his palm.

"It's obvious," Heather said, getting up from the table, "that the lucky guy is you."

It was a mean thing to say since Heather didn't believe it, but when she saw the naked hope and pleasure in Ed's eyes, her anger took over and she told herself he deserved it.

Stupid,
moron,
shit-head
CJ **impossible**
was
sticking
his stupid
gun in her
face again.

EVER SINCE SHE'D WOKEN FROM THAT

dream, Gaia was so distracted, she could hardly remember to breathe regularly or feed herself or put one foot in front of the other when walking.

Ow. She kicked her big toe hard against a ledge in the cracked cement sidewalk and stumbled forward.

She certainly couldn't be bothered to come up with appropriate kiss-ass behavior for the vice principal, which was why she'd sat through detention, which was why she was walking home late.

She arrived at the corner of the park. Cut through or take the long way?

In her state, the right thing to do was go around. How was she going to make the dream happen if she got shot today?

She cut through, anyway. To do anything else was purely against her nature.

Would Sam be at the chess tables today, and if so, what should she say? It was time to get serious about her plan. No more being shy. No more being awkward. Her dream emboldened her.

Oh God, and there he was. She spotted him from the back, playing chess with Zolov. His elbow rested on the edge of the table, and he cradled his head in his hand. The last of the day's sun turned his tousled hair into gold. She could see a bit of his profile, the sensual curve of his mouth.

It was the perfect opportunity to proposition him, but she couldn't seem to make her feet go forward. She called up the dream again, but far from emboldening her, it turned her cheeks red and made her feel very shy. Those were the lips that had made her feel . . .

She heard scrambling behind her and spun around. *Oh, shit.* She took off at a run. CJ was lying in wait, of course, as she certainly knew he would be. Why was she so stupid? Couldn't she give up the death wish for even a day or two? At this rate she *deserved* to die a lonely, bitter, parentless virgin.

She cursed herself as she sprinted through the park and westward toward Sixth Avenue. It would be busy there this hour, hopefully busy enough to lose him.

Gaia raced onto the avenue. *Beeeep! Beeeeeeeeeeeeeep!*

"Get the *hell* out of the *street!*" somebody screeched.

A maroon commercial van swerved to avoid her and plowed into the back of a taxicab. Gaia heard the crumpling of metal. The taxi rear-ended a black Mercedes-Benz convertible. The Mercedes drove up onto the sidewalk and crushed its headlight against a parking meter.

Oh, Jesus. Gaia ducked behind a stopped garbage truck as the air filled with shouting drivers slamming doors and the excited buzz of pedestrians crowding to watch the show. No one was hurt, Gaia was pretty sure of that, and the chaos gave her a second to collect herself. She spotted CJ on the curb, his eyes wildly scanning the street for her.

Don't move, she told him silently. *I'll be right there.*

This was all she needed—a chance to see him without being seen. She noticed with huge relief that he'd stuffed the gun back in his jacket. The sidewalk where he stood had largely emptied of people, who were drawn to the activity a little ways down the street.

Ducking as she crept along, she used the line of stopped cars to conceal herself. She had him directly in her sights, not ten feet away. *Now go!*

She pounced. In a single graceful move she captured both of his arms and wrenched them behind his back. She dragged him several yards off the busy avenue to the relative backwater of Minetta Lane. CJ growled and twisted his body to free his arms. He succeeded, or at least he thought so. The truth was, she was happy to let him come at her as long as the gun stayed out of his hands.

"Bitch," he hissed at her with a snarl. He took a step back to get some leverage, drew back his right arm, and launched his fist at her face. She dodged it easily. She felt relaxed, even—shamefully—a little excited. For Gaia a fistfight against one other person hardly drew a sweat. And CJ was just the kind of asshole she most enjoyed putting in his place.

118

He hauled off again, this time aiming the punch at her stomach. She caught it long before it landed. His exertion threw him so far off balance, she used the offending arm to lay him out on the pavement with the smallest effort.

He quickly found his feet and stood up, bellowing a long string of obscenities. He was squaring off, spitting mad, trying to find some way at her.

All right. It was tempting to linger but not a good idea. Time to close this thing out. He leaped at her sloppily, swinging both arms. She ducked and landed a swift, hard jab in his stomach. He doubled over, unable to breathe. She kicked him on the shoulder and sent him sprawling to the pavement. Now she knelt by his head, wrapped her forearm around his neck, and pulled him up onto her lap. She plunged her other hand roughly into his jacket, feeling around for the gun.

CJ gaped at her with surprise and fear, still unable to catch a breath. He probably thought she was going to kill him. And he did deserve it. What a joy it was to reverse their roles, to have him right where she wanted him. He should have known he didn't have a prayer against her one-on-one. Few people did. That wasn't bragging; it was just a fact. The gun was what threw everything.

"Don't you know better than to open fire in a crowded street, you stupid bastard?" she barked at him. Where was the damn gun? She tightened her grasp on his neck and made her way through his pockets. CJ's dark red wool cap got pushed to the side, revealing his stubbly bald head.

Unpleasant as it was, Gaia jammed her hand down his shirt. She saw the ugly black hieroglyphs carved into the skin of his chest and made a mental note to never, ever consider getting a tattoo.

Okay. Now she was getting somewhere. She felt the cold butt of the gun with her fingertips. What a huge relief. In a rush of hopefulness she felt the possibility of this whole insane episode coming to an end and the world stretching out with her alive in it.

Maybe she could calm down about this sex thing and go about a relationship like a normal human being. Maybe she could take on the search for her dad in a thoughtful and intelligent way.

She gripped the gun, which CJ had secured in the tightly belted waistband of his pants.

Maybe she could—

Gaia shouted in surprise as an arm closed around her own neck. Her thoughts scattered, and she lost her hold on the gun as she was wrenched backward.

"Leave the kid alone!" a voice thundered much too close to her ear. She snapped her head around to look over her shoulder. Less than a foot away was the red face of a very large man in a disheveled suit jacket and tie.

What—?

The large man dragged her back another few feet. By now CJ had sprung to his feet and lightly patted the gun still tucked in his pants.

"Did she get your wallet off you?" the man asked CJ, concern clear in his voice. "You go tell the police all about it, son. There's a squad car around the corner."

Unbelievable. Gaia was speechless.

This guy wasn't a friend of CJ's, a fellow thug from the park, as she'd briefly imagined. This was a suit-wearing, forty-something-year-old, white-collar stranger on his way home from work. This was an angry citizen taking justice into his own hands. A vigilante. He believed she was mugging CJ. He was *protecting* CJ!

What an awful joke. CJ, out on bail, concealing an illegal weapon, had every reason not to seek the help of New York's finest. He only stayed long enough to sneer at Gaia, pull his hat back down over his ears, and smile.

"You're dead!" CJ shouted over his shoulder at Gaia as he took off at a run into the bedlam of the Village on a Friday night.

The big guy was practically strangling Gaia, but she was too miserable at the moment to do anything about it.

"I've heard about girl gangs," the man was saying, not to Gaia, but not to anyone else, exactly. "That kid may not want to turn her in, but you can be sure I'm not letting her go."

Obviously the man meant it because he started

yanking Gaia toward Sixth Avenue. Was there any point in telling him the magnitude of his mistake?

"Um, sir?" She loosened his grip around her neck so she could breathe and speak. "You have to let me go now." She locked her feet on the pavement and stood firm.

He stood up tall and puffed out his chest in indignation, even as he attempted to crush her trachea. He was at least six feet four and very powerfully built. His hair was dark and thinning on top. He looked like an ex–offensive lineman. Unless he was some kind of wretched, hypocritical wife beater, he probably wasn't used to fighting girls.

"Kids like you gotta be kept off the street," the man told her. "I don't want to hear any sob stories. You can save it for the cops."

Gaia sighed. Things were not going her way. "Look, sir," Gaia said reasonably. "I don't want any more violence tonight, but if you won't let me go, I'm going to have to force you, and it could hurt."

The man looked at her in disbelief. Then he laughed dryly. "You're going to hurt *me?*"

"I don't want to. I realize you're just trying to help out. I appreciate that."

He laughed again.

"I'm serious," Gaia said. "Let me go now."

He stared at her with undisguised amusement. "You're scaring me."

"Sorry, then," Gaia said flatly.

She gave him about ten more seconds to withdraw. She actually did feel bad, but what was she supposed to do? She wasn't getting booked and spending several more hours of her life in a police station. It brought back memories of the worst hours of her life. There was just no way.

She placed both of her hands on the man's arm that circled her neck. Without any more force than necessary, she took a deep breath and flipped him over her shoulder onto the ground.

He landed hard, what with being so huge and old. He let out a terrible squawk. As he lay there writhing in discomfort, staring at her as if she'd grown second and third heads, all traces of amusement disappeared from his face. She hoped very genuinely that he would feel better tomorrow.

"Sorry," she said again before she ran off.

"THAT'S HER! THAT BLOND GIRL!"

No More Thinking

Gaia was rounding the corner of Bleecker Street less than sixty seconds later when she heard another commotion behind her. Gaia turned her head partway, and out of the corner of her eye she saw two police-men pointing after her. The big man in the suit had managed to sic the cops on her in record time.

She didn't turn her head any farther or slow her steps. The cops hadn't really seen her face yet, and she meant to keep it that way.

It was wrong and bad to run away from cops, but Gaia was really tired now, and she hadn't done any-thing illegal, except maybe flip the balding guy, but he was strangling her, and he deserved it. Furthermore, she had given him ample warning.

She would just run away from them this one time, she promised herself. In the future she would be extra friendly and helpful to the police.

She was coming up on her favorite deli when she had a brainstorm. The hatch to the basement, a sprawling black hole in the sidewalk in front of the store, was open. She could disappear without having been seen, and the cops would probably be happy to forget about the whole thing. Were they really going to blame a high school kid for roughing up a guy three times her size? She practically dove into its darkness. She pulled the heavy metal doors shut be-hind her and clung to the top of the rickety conveyor belt used to stock the supply rooms. She heard foot-steps banging along overhead. Hopefully they be-longed to the cops.

Ugh. The place was pitch black and smelled awful.

It was unfortunate to be winded and gasping for breath in a place where the air was thick with dust and rotting food. There were certainly rats down below, but she didn't want to think about that too much.

Gaia glanced at the glowing hands of her watch. Five minutes took several hours to pass. At last she opened one of the doors a crack and peered out. Never had New York City air smelled so fresh. No sign of any police.

She opened it another few inches. She was either home free or a very easy target. Still no sign. Time to make her move. She threw open the hatch door and climbed out. Once on the sidewalk, she spun around.

What she saw made her freeze. Her blood seemed to stop in her veins. Black blotches clouded her vision. She put her head down to prevent herself from fainting, and when she looked up again, he was gone.

It wasn't a cop. It wasn't CJ. Who knew where he'd gone? The man she'd thought she'd seen in that split second looked uncannily familiar. He looked, although she was sure she'd imagined it, like her father. It couldn't have been. She was low on oxygen, overtired, overwrought. It couldn't have actually been him. But it shocked her to her core just the same.

On trembling legs she found her way home. She stopped at the bottom of the stoop, trying to regain her breath and her sense of balance. She prayed Ella wouldn't be home yet.

Deep, cleansing breaths. In, one, two, three. Out, one, two, three. She put her hands on her hips and bent her head low to keep the blood flowing into it. She wasn't going crazy. There could be people in the world who looked a little like her dad. Was that so impossible?

It was a crazy night. With all she'd been through, who could blame her for a minor hallucination?

"Say good-bye, bitch."

Gaia choked on her cleansing breath. Stupid, moron, shit head CJ was sticking his stupid gun in her face again. How much more could she take in one night? She was completely beyond reason. She was exhausted and mad and frustrated and totally freaked by the sight of that familiar man.

Without thinking, she shocked both herself and CJ by wrenching the gun right out of his hand and throwing it as hard as she could down Perry Street. She wanted him away from her. Now. That was it.

CJ ran after it.

"Can't you leave me *alone* for a couple of *hours,* you little *shit?*" she screamed after him.

Then she lumbered up the stairs to the front door, carrying with her the discomforting knowledge that in addition to losing her heart and her pride, she had also lost her mind.

The only thing she'd managed to keep was her virginity.

Wearing Patience

"THAT STUPID, STUPID GIRL!" HE paced the floor of the loft, pausing briefly to kick an ottoman out of his way. "Ella, did I not order you to kill that lowlife the same way you killed his friend? What is the problem here?"

Ella glared at the parquet floor. "I said I'm trying, sir."

"Clearly not very hard. You are a trained assassin, need I remind you, and he is a pathetic, imbecilic teenager. Do you honestly need backup?" He beckoned to his two omnipresent bodyguards, who stood at attention several yards away.

"No," Ella said firmly.

He glared irritably at Ella. Was she not adequately frightened of him anymore?

He methodically took a gun out of his drawer, walked over to her, and pressed the barrel to her forehead. "Ella, you know I would as easily kill you as ask you this a third time?"

She didn't meet his gaze. "Yes, sir."

"I've taken some pains placing you with that doormat George Niven, so I'm forced to be patient with you. But know this, Ella. My patience is wearing."

No, she wasn't frightened enough. He fired the gun so that the bullet nearly grazed her nose and ruptured a windowpane with a blast of noise. Ella jumped back in shock. Her eyes were momentarily filled with fear.

There. That was better.

"Trust me, Ella, if something happens to that girl, I will kill you and everyone you have ever cared about. I need Gaia, and I need her alive."

He walked to the wall of windows, watching the dying sun set flame to New Jersey's sky in a lurid show of color.

Perhaps it was time to move forward. Perhaps it was time to bring Gaia in.

HOW LONG HAD HE BEEN SITTING

here? Tom wondered, looking up at the ceiling of the diner absently. Cracks riddled the surface of the plaster, buried under multiple coats of high-gloss light orange paint. The color was the same as the bun sandwiching the burger that sat on his plate, which he hadn't found the appetite to eat.

Clinging

He truly hadn't expected to see Gaia. He hadn't prepared himself for it. Now his fragile hold on life's priorities were shattered once more.

His baby. His child. His and Katia's. His throat ached at the memory of her face. He'd known she'd be grown-up now, much like a woman, but he didn't *know*. He hadn't been ready for it.

He'd always imagined she would grow up to be a beautiful woman, being Katia's daughter, but he was surprised by precisely how. She wasn't petite like her mother. She was tall and lanky, like him. Her hair had stayed that glorious pale yellow. He would have guessed it would fade and darken, as most child hair did, but hers hadn't. It had remained straight and soft looking. Her eyes were still deep, challenging blue. Some blue eyes looked pale and watery—more an absence of color than a color itself. But Gaia's were rich with pigment, a dense, tumultuous, changeable blue.

He'd desperately wanted to go to her. To hold her for just a few minutes. To tell her he loved her and thought of her every hour of every day. He needed her to know that she would never be alone; she would never be unloved as long as he was alive.

And if he had, what would she have said to him? Would she have glared at him in anger? In hurt? Could she ever forgive him for abandoning her?

Tom pulled his eyes back down from the ceiling, pinning them to the chipped Formica table on which his hands rested. What was the use of imagining it? He couldn't hold Gaia. He couldn't talk to her. To contact her would be selfish and put her in greater danger than she could ever know. His presence here at all was a terrible, senseless risk.

Five years ago he'd clung to Katia, and in doing so he'd as sure as killed her himself. He couldn't do that to Gaia. He'd already hurt her enough.

His desire rose to an unquenchable **from** thirst as he burrowed his **the** lips in her soft, **waist** buttery hair— **down**

"GAIA, IS THAT YOU?" ED FARGO

stared at the pretty brunette in the wide-brimmed straw hat, sunglasses, and flowery dress standing in the doorway of his family's apartment.

Condom Shopping

"Yes. Duh," she replied somewhat impatiently.

Ed studied her for another moment in confusion. "Why are you wearing a wig?"

"What wig?" Gaia asked.

"Have you been a brunette all this time and I just didn't notice?" Ed asked, feigning innocent surprise.

Gaia rolled her eyes. "I'm not wearing a wig, smarty-pants. I colored my hair with washable dye," she explained reasonably.

"Oh. Aha. Okay, then."

Ed shut the door behind him and locked it, and he wheeled along next to her down the hallway to the elevator. Gaia, typically, didn't offer any more information.

"Would you mind if I asked why?" Ed asked as the elevator arrived and Gaia pushed him in.

Gaia tapped her foot on the linoleum floor. "What happened to your promise not to ask questions?"

"I meant I wouldn't ask questions about big stuff," Ed said defensively. "Parents, past, unusual abilities. Not hair color. But fine. Don't tell me if you don't want."

Gaia sighed huffily. "Fine, I will tell you. But don't chicken out on me, okay?"

Ed put his head in his hand. "I have a feeling I'm not going to like the explanation very much."

"Okay?" Gaia pressed.

"Okay," Ed replied weakly.

The elevator arrived at the lobby, and the doors opened.

"Remember I told you CJ was out to get me?" Gaia asked, following him out of the elevator. "Well, he's still out to get me, and I'm sick of hiding out in my room. I wanted to go on this errand with you, but I don't want him to open fire again, particularly not at you. So that's why I look like this."

Ed swallowed. He let his wheelchair roll to a stop. "CJ is likely to open fire in the middle of the day?"

"Not if he doesn't recognize me," Gaia said breezily.

"But if he does?" Ed demanded.

"Yeah. Probably." Gaia took hold of the back of his chair and rolled him to the entrance of the building.

"Gaia! What do you think you're doing?"

"You said you wouldn't chicken out," Gaia reminded him, rolling contentedly along.

"I didn't realize my *life* would be in danger," Ed complained.

"It won't be," Gaia assured him without sounding at all convincing.

"Gaia! Stop pushing me! I'm being hijacked here!"

Gaia stopped. She took a breath. "Sorry," she said, like she meant it. She turned him around. "You're right. I'll take you back."

"No. I'm not saying . . . I'm just—" Ed sputtered. Why was Gaia so frustrating all the time? How did she always manage to stay in control of every situation? "Gaia, stop! Just stop."

Gaia stopped. She let go of the chair.

"Thank you," Ed said. He looked around the dull gray lobby with its drab fifties decor and hoped that no one he or his parents knew was within hearing distance of this conversation. "Now, don't roll me anymore."

"I'm sorry," Gaia said. "I really am. I won't do it again."

He glared at her in silence.

"Do you want to come or not come? It's totally up to you," Gaia said solicitously. "I promise I won't *touch* your chair."

She actually looked sweet as she waited for his response. Man, she made a fine brunette. Errrg. He knocked his knuckles against the armrest. Of course he would go with her, even if he *was* going to get shot at. That was the really pitiful thing.

"All right, Gaia," he said after he'd made her wait long enough. He wheeled into the bright sunshine of First Avenue, and she followed. "But slow down, okay? You're making me nervous."

"I'll try. It's just that I've had a rough couple of days, what with not getting killed and all."

"Right," Ed said, wondering how he'd ended up with such a friend.

They walked across the avenue and took East Sixth Street past all the Indian restaurants toward Second Avenue. Ed could smell the curry.

"So where are we going?" Ed asked.

"To buy condoms," Gaia replied.

(Cough.) "To buy"—Ed paused to clear his throat so his voice wouldn't come out squeaky—"condoms?"

"You gotta be safe," Gaia pointed out.

Ed scratched his head behind his ear. "Yes. Yes, you do," he said slowly. "Can I ask who they're for?"

"Me," Gaia said.

"Um . . . Gaia?"

"Yeah?"

"I don't know if you ever got to the unit in health class where they covered this stuff, but . . . uh, condoms are usually intended to be worn by the—"

Gaia punched him on the shoulder playfully but still too hard. "I don't mean I'm going to *wear* one, dummy."

He waited for her to offer some corrected version of her plan, but of course she didn't.

"So you're buying them for a guy?" he tried out.

"Yes," she said.

"And that guy would be . . . ?"

Gaia looked at him over her dark glasses. "Remember how I told you I wanted to have sex?"

"Yeah?" That was a `hard conversation to forget`.

"Well, obviously I'm going to need some condoms," Gaia explained as if she were speaking to a person with a very low IQ.

"Obviously," Ed said. His heart was racing, and he was feeling a bit queasy. He was miserably uncomfortable both with the `remote hope` that Gaia intended to have sex with him and the idea that she was planning to have sex with somebody else.

"Can you tell me who the lucky guy is?" His choice of words made him think of the conversation he'd had with Heather the day before. Had Gaia really written something about him in her notebook? As hard as Ed was trying to sound light and carefree, he felt his life's happiness was hanging on her answer.

"Nope," Gaia said.

Ed felt oddly relieved. "Okay. Let me ask you this. Have you told this person you're planning to have sex with him?" He hated himself for fishing, but he couldn't help it.

Gaia suddenly looked ill at ease. "No, not exactly."

"So you're just going to pounce on him in the dead of night?"

Gaia looked offended. "No. I'm not," she replied stiffly.

"Then what?"

"When I'm ready, I'm going to just go to where he

lives and . . . ask him," Gaia explained a little defensively.

"Just ask him."

"Right."

"I see."

"Does that sound so bad?" she asked. Were her eyes searching, or was he imagining it?

She stopped in front of a discount pharmacy on Third Avenue and gallantly held open the door while he passed.

"Kind of unorthodox, I guess, but not . . . *bad*, exactly."

Gaia was already studying the selection hanging on the wall behind the counter. "So what do you think, Ed?" she asked him, squinting at the labels. "Lubricated? Ribbed? Ultrasensitive?"

Ed tried to breathe evenly. For a girl who'd been concerned about awkwardness a couple of days ago, she was really `taking this in the teeth`. "Jeez, I don't know," he said feebly. He scanned the back wall, which was jam packed with every brand of embarrassing merchandise—birth control, tampons, pregnancy tests, laxatives, hemorrhoid medicine. What sick mind decided that all that stuff went behind the counter where you had to ask for it by name? "You pick."

She pointed out the package she wanted to the cashier man, who wore a sweater vest and a name tag that said, "Hi, my name is Omar." Omar, looking curious and somewhat amused, spent an extra-long time locating Gaia's choice. At last he slapped the bright red box on the counter, and Gaia paid up. Ed realized Omar was giving him approving, `go-get-'em` looks.

"Have fun," Omar said as they left the store.

Ed was certain his face was probably the shade of a ripe strawberry. He suddenly wished he weren't wearing a bright orange tie-dyed T-shirt.

"Do you think the guy is going to say no?" Gaia asked as they started back in the direction of his building.

"I'm not saying that."

"But you're thinking that," Gaia accused.

"No, it's just . . . I mean, look, Gaia, it's not your everyday thing to do to a guy."

Gaia nodded thoughtfully. "I realize that. I do. But I'm a little desperate here. I figure I can stay alive till tomorrow, but maybe not after that. If there's any chance of losing my virginity before then, I've just got to do it. Tonight."

"Tonight?" Ed couldn't hide his shock.

"Yeah."

"Tonight," Ed repeated numbly.

"Yes, Ed. Tonight. Saturday night."

`Ed's brain felt like it was shutting down.`

"So I'm just going to go right to his room and ask. Nicely, of course. I won't insist or anything. And if he seems really reluctant or . . ."

"Freaked out," Ed supplied.

138

"Or freaked out," Gaia allowed, "I'll just tell him the truth."

Gaia paused to let him say something, but when he didn't, she surged ahead. When she was with Ed and her mouth got going, there was no stopping her.

"The truth is good. The truth is your friend. Seriously. I'll just say to him, Look, I'm probably going to get shot in the head tomorrow, and I really want to have sex before I go, so would you mind?"

Gaia looked at Ed again for some response. He couldn't even work his mouth anymore.

"And even if he thinks I'm completely repulsive and would rather have sex with his aunt, well, he probably still won't want to refuse a girl's dying request, will he? What do you say?" She turned to Ed with a genuinely hopeful look on her face.

Ed struggled for words. "I—I say. I say . . . have fun."

The Wrong Girl

"PLEASE TABULATE YOUR RESULTS according to the format Dr. Witchell presented in the lecture on Thursday."

The very droopy-looking kiss-ass teaching assistant droned on as Sam pictured

139

the way Heather would look when she appeared in his room that night.

It was unfortunate that his lab section of biochemistry had to meet on Saturday. It was especially unfortunate on *this* Saturday, when his mind was impossible to contain.

Would she wear that short black skirt that made him drool? Maybe one of those miniature T-shirts she had that showed off her belly button? And what about under it? It probably wasn't a good idea for him to go there right now, but he couldn't help it. He pulled his chair up so his waist pressed against the table and further obscured his lap with his notebook. It was highly embarrassing to get excited in class— something he hadn't done since seventh grade.

He'd made his way into Heather's sexy satin bras before. That was a pleasure he was looking forward to. But it was the new frontier that piqued his interest. Would she wear satin panties to match, like the women in those lingerie ads?

Suddenly he wasn't picturing her clothes anymore; he was picturing himself taking off her clothes. He couldn't help that, either. And as the fantasy evolved he wasn't under the harsh fluorescent lights of a science lab anymore but in his (now almost clean) dorm room in low romantic light (he made a mental note to buy a candle). His body pressed against her soft skin, his hands exploring her luxurious curves. Her soft, dark hair tickled his chest. His lips trailed up her neck and under her chin.

He sighed (almost inaudibly) and kissed the lids of those mysterious eyes, the bridge of her thin, straight nose, the plains of her bewitching face. His desire rose to an unquenchable thirst as he burrowed his lips in her soft, buttery hair—

Sam looked up in alarm. The blissful fantasy screeched to a stop with jarring suddenness. It felt like somebody had ripped the needle off an old vinyl record spinning a Mozart symphony.

He wasn't kissing Heather. Where had this fantasy gone so far awry? Heather didn't have hair or eyes or legs like those. Somehow Gaia had arrived in his reverie uninvited. He should have been jolted, surprised, even repulsed by her sudden presence in his bed, but was he? No. The look and feel of her had sent his desire into some completely new stratosphere.

This was not good. This was very bad. What was he going to do?

"Sam . . . ? Sam, uh . . . Moon, is it?"

Sam blinked several times. It took him a moment to bring the TA's face into focus. When he looked around the lab, he realized that except for the TA, he was all by himself. The class was gone, over. The TA was gazing at him as if he were a particularly puzzling specimen in a petri dish.

"I've kind of got to close up here, if you . . . uh . . . don't mind," the TA pointed out.

"Sure. Sorry," Sam said feebly, trying to coordinate his limbs to lift him out of his chair and walk him out of the classroom. "See you," he said over his shoulder.

Still in a fog, he walked down the corridor of the science building and out into the windy courtyard, where the bright, hopeful afternoon sun was threatened by blotchy gray clouds gathering on the horizon.

Little-Known Facts about me:

The summer before my sophomore year, I fell in love. It was the most idyllic summer you could possibly imagine. My family had rented a house in East Hampton that year. My mom and sisters and I stayed for the whole season, and my dad came out on weekends. Those were the days when my dad's business was doing really well.

Ed Fargo was spending the summer at his aunt and uncle's place just a few blocks away. Ed's folks are teachers, but his aunt is this big-time lawyer with a beautiful house right on the beach.

I was working at the farmers' market in Amagansett, and Ed was working at a surf shop on the Montauk Highway. Ed is a year older. You've met Ed, so you know he's seriously good-looking, funny, charming, self-deprecating, super-sharp, and generally a great guy. He was also an amazing surfer. This all took place before his accident, as I'm sure you've already guessed.

HEATHER

Anyway, our love story would take too long to describe here, but it was the most magical time of my life. Someday I'll turn that story into a romance novel, maybe somebody will even make a movie of it, and I'll earn millions of dollars.

The climax of that summer, so to speak, was a night in August, when Ed and I made love on the beach. The moon was full, and the surf was so gentle, we lay together in it. It was the first time for both of us. It was too perfect ever to be described in words, so I won't try.

One month later Ed was paralyzed from the waist down. He spent the next several months in the hospital and in physical therapy. He lost a year of school. Now he's sentenced to a wheelchair for the rest of his life.

Technically, I didn't break up with him. But I would have. Ed let me off the hook by doing it for me—that's the kind of guy he is. I was under a lot of pressure from my parents and everything. They didn't want me spending my youth taking care of a guy in a wheelchair—a guy they felt no longer had "possibilities."

Ed never acted like he hated me after that. In fact, we're still sort of friends. But in his eyes, when I have the courage to look, I see profound disappointment that can never be repaired or forgotten.

I don't need to tell you my parents love Sam. Gorgeous, brilliant, world-class-chess-playing, premed Sam. I'm only eighteen, but they'd be overjoyed if I married him tomorrow. It would relieve some of their financial pressure, I suppose.

You're probably wondering why I told Sam I'm a virgin. The reason is because Gaia is a virgin. I know it for a fact. I don't want Gaia to be able to give Sam something I can't.

Here's a little-known fact

about Ed Fargo: He has a personal
fortune of twenty-six million
dollars. Probably more now because the settlement came over a
year and a half ago, and money
like that earns a lot of interest. His parents, acting on the
advice (and guilt, I guess) of
his aunt, sued over the accident,
even though Ed begged them not to
and he refused to testify.

Ed won't let anybody touch the
money. He will never tell anyone he
has it. I only know because I read
about the windfall in the newspa-
per—no names, of course, but I'm
one of the few people who know the
strange circumstances of the accident. In fact, I first heard about
the case because Ed's parents con-
tacted me about testifying.

Here's another fact about Ed.
His reproductive organs, to put
it clinically, still work perfectly well. Not that it matters
to me anymore.

Heather
paused at
the door,
hesitant **ready.**
for some
or
reason to
not.
commit
herself to
this strange
night.

GAIA WAS AS CLOSE TO NERVOUS AS

a girl who lacked the physical ability to feel nervous could be. She had taken a long bath and spent hours picking out a bra and underpants that wouldn't be completely embarrassing if revealed. She'd brushed her teeth twice.

Just Go

She spent several minutes naked in front of the mirror, worrying that she was too fat. After she talked herself out of that, she worried she was too skinny—bony limbed, underdeveloped, and flat chested.

She couldn't stop herself from making comparisons to Heather. Her body wasn't as feminine as Heather's. Her breasts weren't as big as Heather's. Her feet were definitely much bigger. Her hair wasn't as thick as Heather's.

Gaia had even reverted to the tactics of a seventh grader by calling Sam to make sure he was in his room, then hanging up as soon as he'd answered.

Now, standing in the middle of the floor, wearing the slinky pink dress she'd "borrowed" from Ella and a pair of heels, she felt like a big, oafish fraud. Why was she even putting herself through this? Sam would take one look at her and tell her to get lost. Why did she think he would be attracted to her? Why in the world would he consider going behind Heather's back for *her*? Even if Gaia *was* going to be out of the picture by tomorrow.

She glanced at her watch. Arg. Urmph. It was

almost eight o'clock. If she didn't leave now, Sam would probably head out for the evening, and she'd go to her grave a virgin.

She took one last look at herself. No, this wasn't going to work. She was no seductress. She wasn't going to fool anybody. She pulled the dress over her head and kicked off the heeled sandals. If she was going to go, she'd go as herself. She'd be honest. She pulled on jeans and a T-shirt and dug her bare feet into her running shoes. She thrust the package of condoms into her bag.

As a safety measure she tucked her hair into a wool cap, which she pulled low over her eyes, wrapped a scarf over most of the bottom of her face, and slipped on a pair of glasses with heavy black frames. Not exactly sexy, but neither was a severe head wound.

Thankfully Ella was out, so Gaia could walk down the stairs like a sane human being. She locked the door behind her and struck out into the cool October night, knowing that this was going to be the greatest single night of her life or a complete and total nightmare.

"THE GREEN OR THE BLACK?" HEATHER

asked her sister Phoebe.

Hesitant
Phoebe leaned back on her elbows on Heather's unmade

bed and sized her up. "The green is prettier; the black is sexier."

"Black it is," Heather said, pulling the close-fitting sweater over her head. "Can I borrow that gauzy dark red skirt?" she asked, scanning the many piles of clothing that covered her floor.

"Big night tonight?" Phoebe asked suggestively.

"I hope so," Heather answered in a way that was mysterious but didn't openly invite further questioning.

On the one hand, it was annoying that Phoebe came home from college almost every weekend. She was a sophomore at SUNY Binghamton and hated it there. She referred to it as Boonie U. and was constantly composing the personal essay for her transfer application. Heather reasoned that if Phoebe spent even half that time on her courses, she could actually make the grades to transfer. Heather didn't mention this to Phoebe, of course. Phoebe's old room had been partitioned off and rented out, so Phoebe stayed in Heather's room, and she was quite the slob. On the other hand, Phoebe had managed to accumulate lots of nice clothes—who even knew how—and usually let Heather borrow them.

"Sure," Phoebe said. She got up from the bed and planted herself in a chair at Heather's vanity table. Phoebe leaned close to the mirror and pursed her lips. "Only it's dry-clean only, so don't mess it up."

"Yes, ma'am," Heather said, locating the skirt and pulling it over her hips. Phoebe was taller, but Heather was a little slimmer. "How does it look?"

"Fine," Phoebe said without even giving her a glance. She was rooting through her capacious makeup bag. "Have you seen my brandy wine lip liner? It's Lancôme, and it cost like twenty bucks. I'm sure I had it when I came last weekend."

Heather ignored her. Phoebe was always losing things and subtly blaming other people.

Heather slipped on her black nubuck loafers and checked her hair and makeup one last time. She felt keyed up and a little shaky. She wasn't sure where excitement ended and nervousness began. She checked her purse again to make sure she had the condoms.

"Okay, Phoebe, I'm taking off. See you later."

"See ya," Phoebe said absently, without taking her eyes from her reflection in the mirror.

Heather paused at the door, hesitant for some reason to commit herself to this strange night.

"Wish me luck," she added in a quiet voice, wishing in a way that this were a night from their innocent past in which the two sisters would practice gymnastics in the living room for hours and try to stay up late enough to watch *Saturday Night Live*.

But Phoebe was already too deeply involved in her cosmetics to respond.

"OUCH. SHIT," SAM MUTTERED, putting his index finger in his mouth. He'd tried lighting the candle, but the wick was buried in the wax, and when he'd dug for it in the hot wax, he'd burned himself.

Sincere

He lit the wick again. It took this time, but the flame was sputtering and underconfident.

He sniffed at the air. Crap. The candle was advertised to smell like vanilla, which he'd hoped would cover any residue of dirty-room odor, but instead it smelled like floor cleaner.

He was nervous. He couldn't help himself. He glanced again in the mirror. It seemed stupid to take pains with his clothing when the whole point of this evening was to be taking them off as quickly as possible. He'd actually brought his khakis with him into the bathroom and taken an extra-steamy shower in the hope of getting out some of the wrinkles. He'd put on his softest oxford shirt and carefully rolled up the cuffs. It reminded him of Christmas Eve. All those hours he spent wrapping and tying up presents, when it was all torn up and discarded in a matter of moments.

It was already after eight. His suite mates had gone out. The place was eerily quiet.

He was ready for this. He wanted it. He wanted Heather. As he repeated those words in his head, he felt like a quarterback in the locker room, revving himself up for a big game.

He conjured up an image of Heather's lush body and felt his hormones starting to flow. And it wasn't just sex that he wanted, although face it, what guy could turn that down? He cared about Heather. He really did.

Sam found himself pacing the small (clean) room, reassuring himself. He wanted to do right by Heather. Her honesty and openness were genuinely touching to him. He wouldn't betray that or ever make light of it. Sure, he'd wrapped himself up nicely tonight, but she was the one giving the gift.

When the knock on the door came, the sound seemed to reverberate in his bones. He went to the door slowly, knowing who it was, of course, telling himself he wanted her fervently and yet wishing in a way it were somebody else.

A Failed Experiment

AGAINST HIS BETTER JUDGMENT, TOM Moore saw Gaia rounding the corner of West Fourth Street and followed at a safe distance. As a father he needed to see her safely to her destination, wherever that was. Then he would get on a plane back to Lebanon and resume his mission, leaving romantic notions and painful memories behind.

Based on her strange outfit, Tom guessed Gaia knew she was in danger. With her remarkable hair stashed away under her hat and a scarf and glasses obscuring her face, she was almost unrecognizable. Gaia was well adapted to taking care of herself, he told himself as he followed her east toward Fifth Avenue. He'd taught her the skills she'd need, and her miraculous gifts more than outstripped his teaching and his own abilities, in truth.

Tom, too, had been a prodigy. He had an extraordinary IQ, almost perfect powers of reasoning, and an intuitive genius for understanding the motivations of the human mind—particularly the criminal mind. He had been virtually fearless until he lost Katia. After that he wore fear like a coat of chain mail every day of his life. Tom sometimes imagined that he represented nature's first—though failed—experiment at an invincible creature. Gaia represented its subsequent and much more perfect attempt.

Gaia paused for a traffic light, and Tom took the opportunity to pull out his cell phone. He pushed two buttons, connecting instantly with his assistant. "We'll fly from the base at nine-thirty," he told him.

It was with some sense of relief that he watched

Gaia approach the door of a large building flanked by stone benches on either side. He could see from the awning that it was an NYU building, a dorm. It seemed a safe and relatively ordinary place for a girl to begin her Saturday night. He chuckled to himself at the pleasure it gave him to think that Gaia had friends and an active social life.

Maybe she would be okay. Maybe she could actually be . . . happy. The thought suffused him with unexpected joy.

Suddenly he was glad he had come. He was reassured. He could imagine his Gaia thriving here in New York. That knowledge would strengthen him for almost any trial.

He was just backing off when a glint of metal caught his eye from across the street. His thoughts and perceptions went into warp speed. It was a young man standing in the shadow of a tree, holding a .44-caliber pistol. The young man brought it up to eye level and trained it directly on Gaia.

Tom was across the street in a fraction of a second, never diverting his gaze from the gun. He was nearing his target, ready to throw his weight into the man, when suddenly the young man withdrew the gun. The young man's gaze was still trained on Gaia, but the hand with the gun hung at his side. Tom pulled up short, backing up against the side of a building to escape the young man's notice. When Tom looked back across the street, he realized that Gaia had already disappeared into the building.

Tom closed his eyes for a moment and caught his breath. Had that gun actually been trained on Gaia? Could he have been imagining the danger to her? With a sense of foreboding, Tom watched the young man conceal the gun under his shirt and stroll across the street, stopping under the well-lit awning. The young man glanced into the building and then took a seat on one of the stone benches. Tom knew he was settling in to wait.

Distress mixed with frustration as Tom took out his phone once again and pushed the same two buttons.

"Make it eleven," he told his assistant in an unhappy voice.

My views on Luck:

Before my accident, I used to think I was the luckiest guy in the world. Then I had my accident, and I sort of believed I deserved it because nobody stays that lucky. I used to think that luck got around to each of us equally. When things went badly, you were sort of saving up for a stretch of good luck. When things went too well . . . You get the idea.

According to this theory, I would be in for some good luck, right? I mean, a guy who's in a wheelchair shouldn't have parents who bicker constantly, for example, or an older sister who's ashamed of him. He shouldn't be abandoned by the girl he believed to be his one true love.

But the theory is wrong. Luck doesn't shine her light on each of us equally. She is arbitrary, irrational, unfair, and sometimes downright cruel. There are people who spend their entire lives basking in her glow, and others never seem to get one goddamned break.

Luck is powerful. Don't mess with her. Accept her for what she is and make the best of it. I can't stand that people are constantly blaming other people when bad stuff happens to them. Somebody trips on a sidewalk, and they sue some innocent bastard for millions of dollars. It's *not* always somebody else's fault. Sometimes it's just luck. Bad luck.

Luck is unpredictable. She's not your friend. She won't stand by you.

Maybe in heaven it's different. I do hope so.

But here on earth, my friend, those are the breaks.

He couldn't
hold back
much longer
without a
really good
reason.

it

SAM HAD A NEW RESPECT FOR

biology. Although his mind floated somewhere near the acoustical tiles on the ceiling, his body did all the things a body needs to do in order to successfully propagate the species.

The Big Moment

He gently, efficiently removed Heather's sweater and expertly navigated her tricky front-fastening bra. He gazed at her lovely breasts hungrily, feeling the blood flow to his nether regions quadruple in under two seconds. He pulled her skirt over her perfectly shaped hips, revealed dark purple satin panties equal to his daydreams, and forced himself not to go further yet.

Biology was exerting so much force, Sam had to battle himself not to remove that last bit of Heather's clothing or to pick her right up off the floor, put her on his bed, and hurtle forward into the main event. But he was a gentleman. He'd toughed it out before, and he could do it again. His older brother once told him that if you found you were undressing the girl *and* yourself, take a break and ask yourself whether you're pushing too hard.

Sam stuck to the advice, although it seemed like hours before Heather got around to removing his shirt. She seemed a bit tentative to him. Not scared, but not entirely sure of herself, either.

"We can stop anytime," he murmured against her ear, although biology was begging her not to take him up on the offer.

"No, I'm good," she whispered back.

She punctuated her point by sliding her hands under the waistband of his khakis. From his perch on the ceiling he heard a moan come from deep in his chest.

Now he saw his pants on the floor and only his blue-and-green-plaid boxers standing in the way of nudity. Soft, delicate lips poured kisses over his chest and stomach.

It was weird. His body was fully aroused and responsive, and his mind was remote. Was there a psychological term for this? Was there a treatment for it? Was this at all what death felt like?

He bitterly wished he could get his mind into the action. He'd picked a fine day for a complete out-of-body experience, he mused ironically.

"Ready?" he whispered, taking her hand and leading her to the bed.

Before taking a step, he studied her expression, waiting for her cue. Her face was flushed and intense, but not exactly the picture of lustful ecstasy. Was she holding back? Was she regretting this?

Or was he projecting *his* feelings onto her?

He took his eyes from her body so that biology would ease its choke hold for a moment. "Are you sure, Heather? We don't have to do anything you don't want. We've got plenty of time."

In response she sat down on the bed, placed a hand on either side of his waist, and pulled him down on top of her. She commandeered his mouth with kisses so he couldn't ask any more questions.

"I'm sure. I'm sure I want to do it now," she said against his ear. Why did her tone suggest more grim determination than arousal? Suddenly he felt her hands on the elastic waist of his boxer shorts, pulling them down. Another moan escaped him. He couldn't hold back much longer without a really good reason.

"I love you," she whispered to his chest. He couldn't see her eyes to gauge the depth of her words.

"Mmmm," he said, knowing that wasn't the right answer.

Apparently she didn't need to hear more. She wriggled out of her own panties and pressed the full length of her naked body against his. His body was pounding with pleasure and anticipation. His mind was surprised by her assertiveness and her . . . hurry. It almost seemed like she was in a hurry.

162

The big moment was upon them, and biology was demanding they surge ahead. Sam felt for the condom on the table by his bed. With her help he put it on. With her guiding, demanding arms he entered her. Again he heard the deep groan thundering from his chest. He heard her breathy sigh. At last his mind was pulled down into the whirlpool. At last the sensations became so fierce and so pervasive, his body and mind joined together. At last he was consumed.

So much so that he didn't notice that a slight breeze from a crack in the door had snuffed the fragile flame of the floor-wax-scented candle.

THE HALLWAY OF SAM'S DORM

Cruel Luck: 1

looked surprisingly like the one in her dream, but Gaia's feelings were different. She didn't feel sexy and bold. She felt insecure and deeply self-conscious.

First she knocked on the outer door that read B4–7. Sam's room was B5, so it had to be through there. While she waited for an answer, she pulled off her wool cap and shook out her hair. She unwound the scarf and stowed the ugly glasses in her bag. Her eyes caught the package of condoms floating at the surface of her bag, and the eager box threw her confidence even more.

Gaia knocked again. She waited for what felt like two weeks, but nobody came. Had Sam managed to slip out between the time she'd called and now? She thought she heard a noise inside. Was it okay to go in? Was it kind of a public room?

The thought of trudging back home to Ella and George's house in defeat, potentially only to be hunted down by CJ, was so unappealing, she turned the doorknob and walked inside.

It was a good-sized room, housing four desks, a minifridge, a hot plate, bookshelves, piles of sports equipment, notebooks, jackets, a couch that looked like it had been retrieved from a dump, and a very large television set. Gaia took a deep breath. No people, though.

Could Sam possibly be in his room? Maybe he was sleeping and he hadn't heard her knock. What if she were to creep in and climb into bed with him? Would he start screaming and call the police? Or would they have a beautiful, semiconscious, dreamlike sexual encounter? Gaia's head began to pound at the thought.

She walked very quietly toward room B5. Her spirits lifted. It was just her luck. The door was open a crack, and she heard a sound from inside. It sounded almost like a sleep sound.

Gaia took another deep, steadying breath. *Do it*, she commanded herself. *You have to try.* She put out her hand and placed it lightly on the knob. The brass sphere was a little wobbly in her palm. She gave it the lightest push and let it swing open.

Physicists were always crowing about the speed of light, but in this case the light from the common room seemed to filter into the small chamber slowly, as though well aware it was not a welcome guest. In this case, light traveled at the speed of dawning horror, of rude awakening, of hopes being dashed—but no faster. Before Gaia's round, naked eyes, the form on the bed was illuminated.

Two forms.

SAM HAD BELIEVED HIS BODY

2 and mind joined together as he made love to Heather. But in truth, they weren't actually joined until several seconds later, when his senses alerted him, in fast succession, to the subtle creaking of the door, the surprising influx of light, and most importantly, the stunned face of Gaia Moore. That was *actually* the moment when his body and mind snapped back into one piece.

GAIA HAD NEVER SEEN ANYBODY

having sex before, so the image was raw, crude, strange, terrible, and electrifying at the same time.

2 1/2

She should have dashed out of there instantly, but her astonishment seemed to lock her muscles, giving her eyes ample time to torture her with the sight of Sam's naked body, poetic even under these circumstances. His long, lean form was cupped against Heather's, their hips joined, dewy sweat shared between chests and arms, their legs a mutual tangle.

But by far the worst moment came when Sam turned and saw her. Her pain was too big to hide, she knew, and scrawled flagrantly on her face. Sam was baring his body, but she was caught exposing her soul. Her secret pain, her crushed hope, her sickly envy, and her queasy fascination were there for all to see. Worst of all, Sam saw her see him seeing all of this.

At last her muscles freed her, and she ran.

It wasn't until afterward that she realized she hadn't bothered to look at Heather. Heather didn't really matter much.

3 WHEN SAM LOOKED AT GAIA'S

face, he thought his heart broke for her, but he realized later that it broke for himself.

HEATHER WATCHED GAIA'S FACE

with a disturbing sense of excitement. As full and complex as Gaia's expression was in that surreal moment, Heather knew she wouldn't forget it.

Heather realized later that she hadn't even looked at Sam's face. Somehow she knew his response without needing to look. At the time, it didn't really seem to matter much.

Just when
she'd settled
herself on
that bench
and he'd
gotten her
temple
between the
crosshairs,
she'd taken
off again.

the

chase

GAIA STRODE DOWN THE SIDEWALK, tears dribbling over her cheeks, past her jawbone, and down her neck, hair streaming in the breeze. Her hat and scarf and whatever were some-place. What did it matter? If CJ wanted to shoot her right now, he could be her guest. In fact, she might ask him if she could borrow his gun.

The Park . . .

At that moment she would have burned her eyes out rather than have to see that picture of Sam and bitch-girl ever again. But now the image was stored in her brain for good. Or at least until one of CJ's bullets came to her rescue. "CJ!" she called out semideliriously.

She walked blindly under the miniature Arc de Triomphe that marked the entrance to the park. She staggered to a bench and collapsed on it. She hid her face in her hands and cried. Her shoulders heaved and shook, but the sobs were noiseless. Why did her life al-ways go this way? Why did it always seem to take the worst-possible turn?

Whenever she made the mistake of caring, of wanting something badly, life seemed to take that de-sire and smack her in the face with it.

What had she done to deserve this? Was it because she was strange? A scientific anomaly? Just plain made wrong? If she had fear, like a normal girl, would she also have been allowed to have a mother and a father and a boyfriend? And if so, was there any way she could go back and renegotiate the deal? Give me fear! she would say. Give me tons of it. Give me extra; I don't care.

No more caring, that was the golden rule. Forget about "do unto others" and all of that crap. Life's one great lesson was: Do not care. Not caring was a person's only real protection.

In the midst of sobs and tears and internal ranting, something made Gaia look up. Afterward, when she thought back, she couldn't say precisely what it was. But for whatever reason, she turned her tear-stained face up at that moment, and a terrible night became a perfectly mind-shattering one.

There, not fifteen feet away, standing against the trunk of a compact sycamore tree, was her father. In that split second she saw that he was thinner than he was five years before, that his face was more lined and angular, that his reddish blond hair was cut very short now, but he was unmistakably her father.

Gaia didn't jump to her feet as the result of any specific thoughts or decisions. One minute she was collapsed on the bench, and the next minute she was running toward him. He didn't run to her with open arms in slow motion the way long-lost relatives do in old movies. He gave her a look that was both surprised and pained, then he took off in the other direction.

Gaia followed him without thinking. She had to. She couldn't have stopped herself if she'd tried.

EXACTLY ON SCHEDULE, GAIA HAD

seen him standing under the tree. They had locked eyes, and she had recognized him. As if on cue, she ran toward him, and he ran away from her. It's what her father would have done.

10th St. & 5th Ave.

Now he would lead her to his loft on the Hudson River, just as he had planned. He was about to meet Gaia face-to-face. Excitement, true excitement, bred in his heart for the first time in many years.

For this great meeting the playing field wouldn't be even, of course. But when was it? He would go into it knowing everything about Gaia Moore, knowing her present, her past, her mother . . . intimately. She would go into it believing he was her father.

CJ CURSED IN FRUSTRATION. HE

was so completely consumed by anger, he couldn't think straight anymore. Just when she'd settled herself on that bench and he'd gotten her temple between the crosshairs, she'd taken off again. He

17th St. & 6th Ave.

stowed his gun before anybody saw him and followed her.

Now he was badly winded, running, walking, dodging throngs of pedestrians, weaving through wide avenues clotted with traffic, staying with her each and every step. Not for a second would he lose sight of her blond hair, which luckily for him `practically glowed in the dark.`

Tonight was his night. He'd make sure of it. This couldn't go on another day. Tarick and his boys had made it clear. If he didn't kill Gaia tonight, he'd be dead by morning.

TOM KEPT THE YOUNG MAN WITH

17th St. & 7th Ave.

the gun clearly in his sights as he ran. Here was an example of why agents were never allowed near the business of protecting their families. Tom had seen Gaia's face when she'd emerged from the dorm building, tear soaked and racked with misery, and he'd stopped thinking like an agent and started thinking like a father. He'd lost a step, screwed up.

Gaia had narrowly avoided a bullet, and now they were on the run.

SAM HAD NEVER PUT ON CLOTHES

faster. He felt disgusting about leaving Heather at such a moment, but his more urgent feeling was the need to catch up to Gaia and . . . what? He had no idea. Make her feel better? Make himself feel better? Tell her he wanted

Back Up a Minute

her desperately, body and soul, and the fact that he'd just been making love to Heather was an odd, irrelevant coincidence? That would be a complete lie, yet also true at the same time.

"Heather, I'm really, really sorry," he said to her numb-looking face as he raced for the door. He wasn't so sorry, however, that he waited for a response or even looked back at her once. He felt disgusting.

The elevator was many floors away. He ran for the stairs instead. He took them two and three at a time, stumbling at the bottom and practically crashing into the serene lobby like Frankenstein's monster. Gaia was gone, of course.

Sam ran to the door and scanned the sidewalk in either direction. No sign of her. Now what? If Sam hadn't felt the frantic pangs of a drowning man, he would never have involved the security guard in his predicament.

"Uh, Kevin, hey. Did you see a girl, a blond girl around eighteen, rush out of here?" Sam asked.

Kevin paused for an infuriating two and a half seconds to consider. "Tall, pretty, crying?" he asked.

Oh God, she was crying. "Y-Yeah, that's probably her," Sam snapped, feeling an irrational desire to cram his hand down Kevin's throat and pull whatever informative words he had right out of there. And Sam *liked* Kevin. He and Kevin talked about the Knicks five out of seven nights a week.

Kevin paused again, savoring his important role in Sam's drama.

"Did you see which way she went?" Sam prodded, wild-eyed.

Kevin sighed thoughtfully. "Coulda been downtown," he said at last. "I'm pretty sure she walked downtown."

Sam was already at the door and out of it. "Thanks, Kevin. I really appreciate it." Most of his thanks were wasted on passersby on Fifth Avenue.

He ran toward the park. Of course she'd gone to the park. Every major event in his brief life with Gaia (with the notable exception of this evening) had taken place in the park.

Suddenly Sam had it in his mind that this was a good sign. If Gaia had gone to the park—their place, really—she would want him to find her there. If she was in the park, that would mean Sam could somehow repair this disaster.

When he caught a glimpse of yellow hair, sagging shoulders, and a face buried in familiar hands on a bench near the entrance, his heart soared irrationally. He would take her in his arms; he didn't care. He would tell her he loved her. How weird was that? But it was what his heart was telling him to do. He did love her. He loved her in a way he'd never come close to loving anything before. He'd known it for a while, even if he was too cowardly to say it or act on it. Now he would cut through all the chaos and defensiveness and confusion. He would take a risk for once in his life.

I love you. I love you, Gaia. The words were on his tongue, he could practically feel her in his arms, and suddenly, without warning, without even appearing to see him, Gaia leaped off the bench and started running.

Sam was destroyed. But he did find a reserve of insanity that pushed him to follow her.

HEATHER SAT VERY STILL ON SAM'S

A Brief Visit with Heather

bed, half dressed, with her chin resting in her hands. The room was dark; the suite was perfectly quiet.

In her mind she knew she felt horribly wronged and betrayed and mistreated by Sam, but her insides felt strangely dry. She felt too dry for tears or any of the really muddy emotions. Why was that, exactly? Why did she feel so oddly calm and lucid?

When she thought of Gaia's ravaged face, she felt a burst of gratification and maybe even joy. They had a word for this in German, her mother's first language. *Schadenfreude*. It meant shameful joy—taking pleasure in somebody else's pain.

Heather knew she should have felt shamed by this, but she didn't. She should have felt shocked and furious at Sam, but she didn't quite. Maybe later.

Maybe she was just numb.

Or maybe in her heart she already knew that Sam had fallen in love with Gaia and that he had never truly been in love with her.

Or maybe it was really all because of Ed. Because of the awful things that happened with Ed, Heather's heart wasn't the soft, supple muscle it had once been.

ED FLICKED OFF THE LIGHT IN THE

And Another with Ed

hallway. He wheeled back into his room and unbuttoned his shirt—his best, softest shirt. On the collar lingered a tiny whiff of the cologne he'd put on after his shower. It brought on a pang of wobbly self-pity, and the self-pity brought on anger and discontent. Self-pity was the single worst feeling there was, particularly if you happened to be in a wheelchair.

He hoisted himself into his bed and struggled to take his pants off his immobile legs. A close second, in the race of worst feelings, was helplessness.

Ed didn't need to brush his teeth. He'd brushed them twice two hours ago.

Why was he so sad? He didn't really think Gaia was going to come, did he? No, not really. Not rationally. But he'd made the mistake of listening, just a little, to the seductive whispers of that rotten, misleading bastard called Hope.

If there was some way Ed could have strangled Hope and put the world out of much of its misery, he would have.

Instead he laid his head down on his pillow and cast a glance at the glowing blue numbers of his clock radio. It was 10:02. Only 10:02. Not so late.

What if Gaia . . . it was still possible. . . . And maybe she . . .

Ed groaned out loud and put the pillow over his head. It did nothing to drown out the whispers.

If her own
father was
leading
her into
an ambush, **hell's**
what **kitchen**
was there
to live
for, anyway?

GAIA'S MIND WAS BLANK. HER existence was all and only about keeping the tall man in the gray sweatshirt—her father, she reminded herself—in her vision. At this point Sam, Heather, and CJ were strangers to her, inhabitants of a different planet.

The fact that her father was running away from her was immaterial. The reasons for his presence here didn't cross her mind. She made no consideration of what she'd do or say when she caught him. Past and future no longer shaded her thoughts.

She wouldn't let him get away. She *would not* let him get away. Her consciousness was only as big as that thought.

Pedestrians, cyclists, cars, trucks, pets passed in an unobserved blur. She didn't pay attention to which streets she took and where they'd lead. Chasing was so much easier than being chased because it required no strategy.

The man—her father—was fast. He was clever. He almost lost her when she collided with the Chinese-food deliveryman someplace on the West Side. Her dad was still pretty nimble for an old guy. But Gaia was unstoppable. She was too focused to feel loss of breath or any ache in her muscles. Her father had trained her too well for him to have any hope of losing her.

Now they were in the West Forties, Hell's Kitchen, she believed it was called, and her father was showing signs of exhaustion. From Eleventh Avenue he peeled off sharply to the left onto a dark side street. Gaia pulled up short and turned to follow. In this creepy neighborhood the streets and sidewalks were virtually deserted. Streetlights were few and far between. She saw that the side street dead-ended into the West Side Highway. Her father had disappeared into a building. Which one, though? A second passed before her fine hearing picked up a thud. The inimitable sound of a closing door. Gaia traced the sound to the door belonging to the last building on the street, one overlooking the Hudson River. Quickly she raced around the corner to determine if the building had a second entrance on the river side. It didn't. She had him.

JESUS, WAS SHE EVER GOING TO

44th St. stop? CJ felt like his lungs were on the verge of collapse. He was in no shape to scramble thirty-some blocks uptown and all the way west to the river, much of it at a dead run.

Gaia was running away from him, but she never

once looked over her shoulder to see him coming. Not even when he'd nearly picked her off on Hudson Street, after she'd collided with the Chinese guy on the bike. He'd locked on her head at point-blank range, and she'd stopped to help the Chinese guy up! The girl had ice in her veins. She wasn't a regular person.

When she turned off on the side street, CJ skidded to a hard stop, almost losing his balance. Gaia slowed down, then walked to the entrance to the building at the very end of the street and stopped. CJ didn't move from the corner. He felt his heart pounding like a jackhammer. But now it wasn't just exhaustion. It was excitement, too.

He secured the gun in both hands. He brought it up almost to eye level. Why wasn't Gaia moving—getting her ass out of there? Didn't she know he was there? She was crazy! She was a dead woman.

He tensed his right index finger on the trigger. "This is for Marco," he whispered. And with a huge, heady surge of accomplishment, he pulled the trigger and blew her away.

TOM MOORE WATCHED THE YOUNG gunman from a distance. With deep concentration he observed the young man aim the pistol, aiming his own weapon almost simultaneously. He pulled the trigger and heard two explosions, a fraction of a second apart. With fear spreading through his heart he watched the young man go down. It was a good wound. Enough to scare a guy like that off. For now, he was out of the equation, and all that mattered was Gaia. Tom bolted around the corner in flat-out panic.

Gaia was alive. She was standing at the entrance to a building, looking around to see whence the shots had come. She was unharmed. She didn't even appear particularly concerned. Had she any idea how close that bullet had come to ending her life?

Tom ducked out of sight again. With relief flooding his body, he slid to the pavement and allowed himself a moment of rest to slow his speeding heart. Then he took out his phone and connected with his assistant. "There's a man down. I need you to report it to 911. Make the call untraceable."

SAM WAS WEARY AND CONFUSED and

Gaia's Back

fast losing his grip on reality. He'd chased Gaia for at least two miles of congested city streets up to this godforsaken neighborhood and onto a side street as dark and empty of people as a New York City street could be. What was she thinking? Did she have some plan in mind? And was he crazy, or was there more than one other guy following her?

What was Gaia into now? What had she really come to tell him when she'd barged into his room tonight? Nothing was clear to him anymore—except that Gaia was a source of astonishing complexity and trouble, and of course he knew that already.

Sam staggered along the street, catching a flitting glance of Gaia's back disappearing into an old loft building that faced the river. Now what the hell was he supposed to do?

He didn't pause to answer his own question. He just followed her, of course. He hoped she wasn't leading them both to their deaths. And at least if she was, he hoped he would get a chance to tell her that he loved her (in addition to finding her stupendously annoying) before he went.

GAIA FOLLOWED HIM UP THE STAIRS

on silent feet. Did he know she was still behind him? Did he know she could hear his footsteps perfectly well in the darkness? She was certain her father could have evaded

Her Father

her more skillfully than this. Was it possible he wanted her to find him after all? What could it mean?

Complicated questions were filling up the purposeful blank that had been her mind. Eleven floors up, he exited the staircase. The heavy cast-iron door banged to a close behind him. She waited a second before following.

This had the feeling of an ambush. Gaia knew she should be cautious and prudent, but on the other hand, if her own father was leading her into an ambush, what was there to live for, anyway?

She walked through the door and found herself suddenly in a vast, well-lit loft. The ceiling soared twenty feet above her, and the floor under her feet was highly polished parquet. Enormous floor-to-ceiling windows spanned the entire wall facing the river. She could see the lights of New Jersey across the way and a garishly lit cruise boat churning up the Hudson.

She blinked in the light, regained her bearings, and turned around. There, standing before her, not ten feet away, was her father. He wasn't running from her any longer. He stood still, gazing into her face.

"Gaia," he said.

The raw pain
that lived
hidden
inside her **not**
every **nothing**
day of her
life had
broken free.

GAIA'S HEART WAS VOLCANIC.

Tears threatened to spill from her eyes.

It was really him. He was here with her. For the first time in almost five years she had before her the thing she'd yearned for most.

A Soulless Viper

In those long, empty years she'd hardened her heart against him with anger and distrust, commanding herself not to care, not allowing herself the hope that he would ever come for her.

But now, in his presence, her heart's protective shell was cracking and threatening to fall away. She'd been so strong, so capable for all that time, and now she felt that the pressure of the misery and frailty and helplessness built up over those lonely years could flatten her in a torrent of sorrow and self-pity.

She was like the toddler who'd lost her mother in the grocery store, facing miles of grim, dizzying aisles and shelves with numb courage, not allowing herself the luxury of tears until she was back in her mother's arms.

Now Gaia's tears distorted her father's familiar features, the blue eyes so much like her own. It brought upon her wave after wave of memories that she hadn't allowed herself since he'd disappeared.

Her father scrupulously drawing castles when she loved castles, horses when she loved horses, boats when she loved boats. Making her waffles every Saturday morning through her entire childhood as she sat on the counter and told him stories. Teaching her algebra, basic chemistry, martial arts, gardening, marksmanship.

He was teaching, always teaching her, but he made it fun. On Mondays he would speak to her only in Russian, and she and her mother would make blintzes and potato latkes for dinner. On Tuesdays they'd speak only in Arabic, and she and her mother would make kibbe and hummus and stuffed grape leaves. He and her mother took her on hikes in famously beautiful places all over the country to teach her about the natural world.

Most other fathers Gaia knew were good for one game of catch on Sunday after the NFL games had ended. Gaia's was different.

Now Gaia's father took a step closer. She didn't move.

That blissful childhood was what made it almost impossible to survive the night her mother was murdered and her father disappeared. She needed him and missed him so desperately, crying for him every single night, not understanding at first that he was really gone. And it wasn't beyond his control, the way it was for her mother. He was still alive. He chose something else in his life over her, and even when she became so severely depressed that she could barely eat or sleep or talk for weeks and then months at a time, still he stayed away. He never once called her or wrote. She wanted to die then just so her father would know that he had broken her heart.

Could she ever forgive him for that?

He took another step closer. And another.

His face was close and vivid now. A question hovered in his eyes.

Gaia's heart was a war zone. On the one side was the happiness and devotion her father gave her for her first twelve years. On the other was the brutal neglect for the past five. Which side was more powerful? Would Gaia's love or the anger win out?

She was watching his face very closely.

"Gaia," he said again, tentatively. He reached out to her.

Suddenly the battle shifted. Gaia wasn't sure exactly why. It was something in the way his mouth moved, something indescribably subtle, that made her know that this man was different than the one she'd adored above everything else for twelve years. Something fundamental had changed between the way he was then and now. She couldn't put her finger on it.

The anger surged forward in a fierce offensive, beating back the love with ruthless energy. The victory in battle was so quick and so decisive that when her father came another step closer and reached out his arms to embrace her, Gaia recoiled. Feeling the brief touch of his hands on her shoulders, she experienced no warmth, no affection. Nothing.

Well, not nothing. Anger.

She experienced such powerful anger that she shoved him away from her. "I don't want to see you," she told him.

The anger was building. It was terrifying. The raw pain that lived hidden inside her every day of her life had broken free, and she couldn't control it. She shoved him again, harder this time.

There was sadness and confusion in his face as he stumbled backward, or some semblance of it. She couldn't tell. She didn't know this man. His expressions weren't familiar to her.

She drew back her arm and connected her fist with his jaw. It made a satisfying crack. It was horrible, unspeakable of her to do this, to treat her own father this way.

And yet his expression conveyed no pain. He never took his eyes from her.

She was hauling off for another blow when her arm caught behind her. She spun around and realized for the first time that there was another person in the room. Over her shoulder she saw a tall, very broad man with dark clothing, short dark hair, and a completely blank expression.

Who was this? she wondered distantly, from beyond her rage.

The man held Gaia's arm tightly and twisted it behind her back.

What could her father have meant by this? Gaia wondered, staring at him in indignant disbelief. Was this some kind of ambush after all?

It didn't matter. The oversized man provided an opportune release for Gaia's exploding rage. With some zeal she broke his grasp. Instantly she grabbed a fistful of his hair in one hand and shoved her other hand under his armpit. She positioned her legs for the greatest leverage and swung the son of a bitch over her shoulder, laying him flat out on the wood floor.

She waited for him to scramble back up to his feet before she buried another jab in his stomach and kicked him brutally in the chest.

She was dangerous now. She wasn't in control. She had to put him away before she really did harm. She calculated the exact spot on his neck and struck fiercely with the heel of her hand. The man crumpled to the floor without a glimmer of consciousness, just as she'd expected. He'd wake up in a while. He'd be fine. It was her own wildfire temper that caused her concern.

Her father watched her intently. Beseeching her. She couldn't look at him anymore. If she didn't get out of there, she would do something she would truly regret.

"It's too late. You stayed away too long," she muttered to him as she turned and walked away. He was no longer her handsome, magical father; now only a pale reminder of sickening betrayal and loss, she needed him out of her sight.

She wished he were dead. That way she could treasure the time she had with him. She could carry on in life with the belief that love was real and happiness could be trusted. Now that cherished time, the foundation of her existence, was fatally poisoned by the knowledge that her beloved father had been a soulless viper all along.

TOM MOORE STOOD SWEATING IN

The Dark Half the dark stairwell on the eleventh floor of the largely abandoned loft building. He had a terrible feeling about this. Why had Gaia come to this place? He felt certain there was grave danger here. He sensed it so strongly, his brain clouded with dark, impenetrable fear. He hadn't had this feeling in a long time.

He was preparing to follow her when he heard the

metal door creaking open just a few feet away. He hurled himself backward, concealing at least most of his body behind dusty boxes in the corner of the landing. He crouched there silently.

Gaia staggered through the door and into the stairwell. Her face displayed pure psychic pain. He stopped breathing as she walked within inches of him. Clearly she didn't see him because she continued down the stairs.

Tom felt as if his heart were being ripped from his chest. This was too hard, being near Gaia, seeing her pain, and not being able to help. But he was involved now, and how was he ever going to pull away again?

He knew he would follow her, but before he did, he needed to see what was beyond that stairwell door. Gaia had emerged physically unharmed, but nonetheless something had destroyed her in there.

He had a bad feeling about it. A black curiosity. Even as he crept to the door, he advised himself against it.

He opened the door with ultimate gentleness, wincing in anticipation of the slightest creak. He pulled it open about a foot and took a deep breath. Slowly, silently he peered into the giant loft, his hand poised on the trigger of his gun.

Tom's glance lighted ever so briefly on a man of his own age and build sitting in the middle of the floor, elbows resting on knees, chin resting in hands, silently contemplating.

That man sitting on the floor was exactly Tom's build and exactly his age—to the hour. His face was more familiar to Tom's than any other, and yet Tom flew from the scene with the singular horror of a man who has seen the dead rise and walk.

Tom knew it was the man referred to, in his short, explosive life among the terrorist underground, as Loki, after the Norse god of the netherworld. But he also knew that the man's given name was Oliver Moore and that he was supposed to have died five years ago.

It was Tom's alter ego, his dark half, his brother.

"YOU LET HER GO?" ELLA ASKED IN

If You Love

Something . . .

disbelief, returning to the loft from the floor below.

Loki said nothing. He sat there, meditative.

"After all that, you let her go?"

It was a great failing of Ella's that she couldn't keep her temper under control. She was self-destructively trying to get a rise out of him, and he wasn't in the mood to play. Ella made a grave error in allowing her dislike of Gaia to get the best of her.

For a man who had risen above (or perhaps fallen below?) his emotional impulses long ago, it was rather confounding to feel the sting of Gaia's rejection. He should have been delighted to see the rage and hatred she held for her father—or a man she believed to be her father, at any rate. Instead, in some primal way, he longed to see love in her eyes, no matter who she believed him to be. She was his daughter after all, genetically if not actually. She was the child of the woman he'd loved. In all of the sordid, black history between him and Katia and his brother, Gaia was the prize, and he meant to win her.

"You've lost her now," Ella prodded sullenly.

Loki stood and stretched. He walked toward the windows, admiring the sparkling panorama with fresh eyes. Suddenly he felt enormously hungry, like he'd woken from a very long sleep.

"Until Monday, perhaps," Loki informed her with a careless yawn.

"And why will she be back then?" Ella demanded snappishly.

Loki stood inches from the window, staring out, his hands pressed against the cold glass. He was in no particular hurry to answer Ella. He studied the dark precarious cliffs of New Jersey's Palisades for a long time.

"Because I've detained a certain friend of hers. We'll keep him. Weaken him for a day or so. On Monday morning Gaia will learn that if she doesn't come for him when I wish, I will murder him."

Bad Choice

SAM LAY ON THE CONCRETE FLOOR, feeling the thumping ache in his shoulder and ribs, dully considering the pale shaft of light that crept into the far side of an otherwise black space. Where was he? Where was the light coming from? Why had he come here, and who wanted to imprison him?

He hadn't caught up to Gaia. He had no idea where she'd gone. But the insidious suspicion had taken root in his mind that she had led him here just to be beaten up and held captive by two large men in ski masks. Blind, lovesick moron that he was, he'd chased her right into a trap.

Why, though? What had he done? Who were these people, and what could they possibly want from him?

He heard the wail of sirens coming close and wished without much real hope that maybe they were coming for him.

This was a truly depressing twist. It was so awful that a part of Sam—not a part relating to his shoulder or ribs—almost wanted to laugh.

He'd had a choice between a safe, loving girlfriend and a seamy, mysterious troublemaker, and whom had he chosen? He had abandoned the culmination of a long-desired sexual encounter for a mad dash through city streets and the privilege of getting beaten up and locked up in a deserted building on the far West Side.

He had a choice, and he'd chosen wrong.

GAIA'S LIFE FELT BLEAKER AND
more desolate than the trash-strewn street where she walked. In one night the few joys she'd had or hoped for were obliterated. Her father—the idea of her father—was irretrievable. She had no choice but to accept now that Sam would never be hers. In her misery

Being Brave

she allowed herself to imagine the scene between him and Heather after she'd run off. Sure, they were embarrassed, but once they got over it, they probably had a good laugh at her expense and got back to business—Sam more passionately than before in his joy and relief to have Heather in his bed and not a psychotic miscreant like Gaia.

She walked slowly down the forsaken street, wondering in the back of her mind where CJ was with his gun. She was ready for him now. Plans 1 and 2 had crashed and burned with equal horror. Not a single hope had survived the collisions. She officially had nothing to live for.

Chill winds blew off the Hudson. She was probably cold, she realized, but she was too numb to register it.

She looked around. Wasn't it just her luck that even CJ disappointed her when she wanted him?

Well, she reasoned, she could always load up her pockets with rocks and wade into the Hudson. She could always walk into the screaming traffic of the West Side Highway. She could find her way to the roof of any one of these buildings and leap off. It's not like her demise was dependent on CJ. *Suicide is the most cowardly act,* a voice inside Gaia's head reminded her. Where had she heard that?

For some reason, the smell in the air reminded her of the smell off the lake at her parents' old cabin in the Berkshires. Who knew why. This was gritty urban water, and that was pure mountain runoff.

For some reason, the smell reminded her of her mom, and the memory of her mom magically brought an image into her mind. It was her mom's face, clear and sharp—shaded by Gaia's raw feelings, maybe, but otherwise accurate. It was the way her mom looked dangling her bare feet off the dock, watching Gaia's attempts to fish for dinner, although she knew perfectly well that Gaia would end up throwing every single fish back into the lake.

It made Gaia's heart come back to life a little because this was something approaching a miracle. Gaia could never remember her mother's face clearly. It drove her crazy that she couldn't. And yet here, in the midst of Hell's Kitchen, was Katia's beautiful and beloved face.

And for some reason, seeing her mother clearly right now reminded Gaia of something else.

Although she had lost the two things she longed for, it somehow opened up the opportunity for something she wanted even more. She had the chance to keep on living, even though she didn't think she could.

At the moment it felt to Gaia like a chance to be brave.

here is a sneak peek of Fearless™ #3: RUN

The dream is thick in my eyes, and I want to wake up but I can't. The dream holds me in, grasping me with its sweaty hands.

I am alone, walking through darkness on a sidewalk that wavers in and out of being. When it is solid beneath my feet, I can walk quickly, and I am elated and excited to reach my destination. But then the darkness swirls, eating the sidewalk, and I drop, spiraling downward, until the ground returns. Objects begin to appear in my peripheral vision—street signs, mailboxes, a flight of stairs. I know them. They remind me that I am on my way to Sam.

His dorm is in sight now—tall, much taller than any other building anywhere ever, and all the windows are dark but his. His glows with the faintest pearl-pink light. I don't know how I know it's his room, but I do. So I jump.

And I'm rising, up, up into the night sky. A huge wind meets me, carries me toward the building. I

am being placed down gently inside
the dorm, at Sam's door. In the
dream, I step away from myself,
just to get a look at my face, to
see what real happiness looks like
when I'm wearing it.

Then I hear the noises. Noises
coming from behind the door—
sounds like soft growling, and
deep sighs, sounds which seem to
caress each other. I open the
door and whisper, "Sam?" and the
whisper echoes like an explosion,
and there they are.

They. Them. Him. Her. (Not me.
I'm just looking.)

The wind returns, fiercely,
pummeling me. Funny, it only
flutters Heather's hair a little,
making her look like some supermodel in a fashion photo.

And Sam, he's all tangled up
under her, or around her, or . . .
well, they are entwined. And even
though I don't have a whole hell
of a lot of experience in this
area, I know what they've been
doing to get into that position,

and believe me, it wasn't a game of Twister.

So I scream. It's a gargley noise, a deep, disgusting bellow. I look down at the floor, and scattered around my feet are all these broken shards of something brilliant red, glassy, shiny. Looking at them makes me feel strangely empty. It takes me a moment to realize that these are the pieces of my broken heart. (One corny, cliché image per dream is allowed.)

Then I look back up at Heather; needless to say, I really want to kick her ass. But suddenly, she's no longer the willowy supermodel she was a moment ago. She's changing before my eyes, morphing into a hideous creature, some kind of huge, mutant insect, with a bulging skull and spiney legs, and curved fangs, which are about to puncture Sam's throat.

My first thought: Serves him right.

My second thought: You can't
lose your virginity to the guy if
the Heather Bug eats him whole. So
I reach out to take his hand . . .

And he reaches out for mine . . .

And our eyes meet. It's like
heat lightning, I swear. Things
are looking up.

So I tell the Heather Bug to
disappear, and since it's my
dream, she does.

And I make my way across the
room to Sam. He's telling me I'm
beautiful, and I'm a killer chess
player, and that he wants me.

Wants me. I close my eyes, and
I'm thinking, the feeling's mutual.
And then it's me, tangled up with
Sam, and we're kissing, and somewhere in the dream, my nerve center
registers a feeling it doesn't recognize in real life.

Fear.

Fear that he might be disappointed. Fear that when all is said
and done, he'll choose Heather anyway, even if she is a bug.

But the fear melts away, because

in the dream, Sam whispers, "I love you, Gaia."

Then—BAM—back to nightmare mode. Because I've just opened my eyes, and I'm back out in the dark on the sidewalk and I'm running.

Running after someone who looks just a little too damn familiar.

My father.

And since it's me in my dream, I do the one thing in this world I know I'm really good at.

I throw a punch that knocks the breath out of him, and sends him stumbling backward for miles, and miles, and miles . . .

And I wake up.

Crying.

One of his
eyes was
black-and-
blue,
swollen   **save**
shut, and he   **sam**
looked
frighteningly
pale. Weak.

GAIA HAD JUST STEPPED OUT OF

the shower, when she heard his voice floating up the stairs to greet her. She wrapped a towel around herself, went to the landing, and leaned into the stairwell.

You've Got Mail

"Ed?"

"Yeah."

"What the hell are you doing here?"

She heard him chuckle. "Fine, thanks, and you?"

Gaia smiled in spite of herself. "Sorry. I had sort of a rough night."

"What else is new?"

She imagined him shaking his head at her.

"You can tell me all about it over breakfast," he called. "I brought bagels."

"Really?" Her stomach grumbled loudly. One thing this city had going for it—the authentic, fresh-out-of-the-oven bagels. They almost made up for the high price of Apple Jacks.

"Yeah. So c'mon down."

"I'm totally naked, and I'm dripping wet!" Gaia yelled, wishing Ella hadn't left ridiculously early this morning so she could be shocked by this exchange. At least she'd taken George with her. The last thing Gaia would want to do was give her sweet old guardian a heart attack.

"I repeat," said Ed, chuckling again, "**c'mon down!**"

Gaia rolled her eyes, trying to ignore the flirtatious

undertones of the remark. Five minutes later, she'd slipped into her most worn cargo pants and a gray T-shirt and was on her way downstairs, her hair spraying drops of water all over her shoulders. On the landing, she paused to study the familiar snapshot that hung in a frame there on the wall—the shot George had taken so long ago of Gaia and her parents. Gaia had tried to get rid of it, but Ella had insisted it remain. Gaia squinted at the photo, looking hard at her father.

Her father. She'd seen him two nights ago. Two nights.

And he'd disappeared—again.

Her stomach churned, both with confusion and sadness. Why had he run from her? Why had he shown up in the first place?

Was it some paternal sixth sense that dragged him back into her life? Did he somehow know she'd been on the verge of losing her virginity, and he'd crawled out from whatever rock he'd been hiding under all these years to give her a good, old-fashioned, heart-to-heart talk on morality, safe-sex, and self-control?

Or was it just one more whacked-out coincidence in her life?

She leaned closer to the photo and stared into his eyes.

They were soft, kind, intelligent eyes—and the smile was genuine. The man she'd met on Saturday night had not seemed genuine at all. The warmth and gentleness she saw in the picture had been missing from the man who'd approached her that night. He was different, somehow. Lesser.

"I guess abandoning your kid and living on the run takes a lot out of you," she muttered, heading down the hall.

In the kitchen, Gaia was met by the heavenly aroma of fresh bagels and hot coffee. Ed, who had positioned his chair close to the table, looked up from spreading cream cheese on a poppy seed bagel. "You didn't have to get dressed on my account."

She was annoyed at the blush his grin brought to her face. "Shut up."

"Do you think it's kismet that this place is handicap accessible?"

Gaia raised an eyebrow. "It's either kismet . . . or the building code."

"I'm serious," said Ed. "Do you have any idea how many places in this damn city aren't?"

She felt a pang of pity, but squashed it fast. "So what's kismet got to do with it?"

"You happen to live in wheelchair-friendly digs. I happen to be in a wheelchair." Ed shrugged. "It's like the universe is arranging it so that we can hang out."

"The universe clearly has too much time on its hands." She sat down and pulled her knees up, leaning them against the edge of the table.

"Like lox?"

"Not especially."

3

"Then I'm glad I didn't buy any." Ed pushed a steaming cup of coffee across the table toward her. "Three sugars, no cream, right?"

Gaia nodded, refusing to be charmed by the fact that he remembered, and took a careful sip. She could feel him staring at her.

"You look like hell," he said, shaking a lock of brown hair back off his forehead. "I mean, in a gorgeous, sexy, fresh-out-of-bed sort of way. But still, pretty hellish."

"Thank you, I try." She took another, bolder sip of the hot coffee. "I told you, I had a rough night." Gaia paused, letting the steamy liquid warm her from the inside. "Make that a rough weekend."

"Now we're getting to it," Ed said, rubbing his hands together. "You were unsurprisingly un-findable yesterday, Gaia. So let's hear it." He broke off a piece of bagel and popped it into his mouth. "Who was the lucky guy and how did the ceremonial shedding of the chastity belt go?"

Gaia ignored the bile rising in her throat, picked up a marble bagel, and took a gigantic bite. There was a reason she'd avoided Ed all day yesterday—the need to avoid forced emotional spillage. "Subtlety isn't exactly a talent of yours, is it, Ed?" she said with her mouth full.

"Look who's talking."

He had a point there. She studied Ed for a moment—the just-this-side-of-scruffy hair, the eager-yet-wary brown eyes, the dot of dried blood on his chin where he'd cut himself shaving. Gaia hated that she had to talk about this, but she did. She'd sucked Ed into the whole sorry situation when she'd confessed her virginity. He might as well know the truth.

Gaia closed her eyes. Shook her head. Sighed.

"It didn't happen," she said.

Ed dropped a knife onto the floor with a clatter. "It didn't?"

"Ed!" She opened her eyes and glared at him. "Think you can sound just a little more amused by that?"

"Sorry it didn't work out for you." Ed cleared his throat and she could swear he was stifling a grin behind his steaming coffee. "So what happened?"

Gaia took another aggressive bite of bagel. "Let's just say somebody beat me to it."

"Shut up!" Ed's eyes opened wide. "Gaia, you have to tell me who we're talking about here. You can't keep me in this kind of suspense. I have a weak heart."

"You do?" Gaia asked, reaching for her coffee.

"No," Ed admitted.

"It was Sam Moon."

A sudden shower of chewed bagel bits pelted Gaia's arms. "God, Ed! Food is to go in the mouth. *In*," Gaia said, brushing off her arms.

"You walked in on Sam and . . . Heather?" Ed choked out while simultaneously attempting to wipe his mouth.

"Ironic, isn't it?" Gaia asked, flicking one last bagel wad off her elbow.

Ed looked as if he were watching his life flash before his eyes—backward and in 3D stereo surround sound. Gaia had never seen skin so pale before in her life. She'd forgotten for the moment that Heather meant something to Ed as well. A big something.

"Man." Ed let out a long rush of breath. His eyes were completely unfocused. "That had to suck."

"Could've been worse," Gaia said with a half-hearted shrug. It had been worse. The night had been full of mind-bending surprises. But she wasn't about to tell him that. No need to burden Ed with her highly dysfunctional family matters over breakfast.

"Worse than walking in on the object of your seduction in bed with your mortal enemy?"

Gaia nodded, but she was saved from expanding on her comment by the sound of the phone ringing.

Ed reached behind him, snatched the cordless from the counter, then slid it across the table to Gaia. She hit the button and held the receiver to her ear. "Hello?"

At first, nothing.

"Hello?"

"Gaia Moore?"

Her eyes narrowed. "Yeah? Who is this?"

The voice was distorted, like something from a horror movie. "Check your e-mail." It was a command. Maybe even a threat.

She felt as if ice were forming in her veins. "Who the hell is this?"

"Check your e-mail," the voice growled.

The line went dead.

Gaia was on her feet, running for George's computer, which, luckily, he always left on. When she reached the den, she flung herself into the chair and punched at the keyboard. Ed, maneuvering his chair through the rooms, appeared soon after.

"What's going on?"

Gaia was too morbidly curious to bother answering Ed's as yet unanswerable question. She clicked the "Read Mail" icon and stared at the screen as it choked out the early cryptic shadows of a video image, tapping her fingers impatiently on the mouse as the picture emerged . . . slowly . . . slowly . . .

It was someone with his back to her, hunched forward. His surroundings were vague, too much light. Gaia reached for the speaker, in case there was audio. There was. Static, at first. Distant, fuzzy, then clearing.

"Maybe it's Heather, playing a joke," offered Ed. "To get even."

"I don't think so," said Gaia, her voice tight.

And then she heard his voice . . .

"Gaia . . . ?"

Her heart seemed to freeze solid in her chest. No, no, no, no.

But the voice through the speaker repeated itself. "Gaia."
No! "Sam?"

As if he'd heard her, he turned to the camera, and

suddenly there was Sam's face on the computer screen. One of his eyes was black and blue, swollen shut, and he looked frighteningly pale. Weak.

Ed angled his chair close to the desk. "Oh, shit."

Sam's face vanished, replaced by a blank screen, and then there was a blast of static from the speakers, as the same distorted voice addressed her. "Gaia Moore. You can see from this footage that we have a mutual friend. Sadly, he's not feeling well at the moment. Did you know Sam is a diabetic? No, I would imagine you didn't . . ."

Ed stared at the blank screen. "Who the hell is it?"

Gaia shushed him with a sharp hiss, as a graphic began to appear on the screen—a message, snaking its way from the right side, one letter at a time: C . . . A . . . N   Y . . O . . . U

The voice continued as the letters slid into view. "He's well enough for the moment but around, oh, say, ten o'clock this evening, he'll be needing his insulin, quite desperately. And that, my darling Gaia, is where you come in. You must pass a series of tests. If you do so by ten o'clock tonight, we will free Sam. If you do not . . ."

The graphic slithered by: S . . . A . . . V . . . E

" . . . He will die!"

S . . . A . . . M . . . ?

For a moment, the question trembled there on the dark screen. CAN YOU SAVE SAM? Then the letters went spinning off into the infinite background, and another message appeared in an eye-searing flash of brightness. It read:

> You will find on your front step a videotape. You will play it during your first-period class. DO NOT view the tape prior to showing it in school.

Without warning, the e-mail broadcast returned, showing a close-up of Sam's beaten face, frightened eyes, his mouth forming a word, and the word came screaming through the speaker in Sam's voice.

"Gaia!"

Then, nothing. The image and the audio were gone, and the computer whirred softly, until George's sickening screen saver—a scanned-in photo of Ella—returned to the screen.

Gaia sprung up from the chair, and flew to the front door, which she flung open. The early-morning October air sparkled and the neighborhood was just coming alive with people on their way to work and school. Gaia paid no attention. Her eyes searched the front stoop until they found the package.

She lunged for it.

Gaia had no idea who had done this. She had no idea why. But she wasn't about to ask questions.

Not with Sam's life on the line.

Some secrets are too dangerous to know . . .

R O S W E L L
H I G H

In the tiny town of Roswell, New Mexico, teenagers Liz Parker and Max Evans forged an otherworldly connection after Max recklessly threw aside his pact of secrecy and healed a life-threatening wound of Liz's with the touch of his hand. It turns out that Max, his sister Isabel, and their friend Michael are surviving descendants from beings on board an alien spacecraft which crash-landed in Roswell in 1947.

Max loves Liz. He couldn't let her die. But this is a dangerous secret he swore never to divulge - and now it's out. The trio must learn to trust Liz and her best friend Maria in order to stay one step ahead of the sheriff and the FBI who will stop at nothing in hunting out an alien...

Available NOW from Pocket Books